D0211550

IC LIBRARY

Sacramento, CA 95814

09/15

WITHDRAWN FROM CIRCULATION

LINCOLN'S BILLY

LINCOLN'S BILLY

Tom LeClair

THE PERMANENT PRESS
Sag Harbor, NY 11963

Copyright © 2015 by Tom LeClair

All rights reserved. No part of this publication, or parts thereof, may be reproduced in any form, except for the inclusion of brief quotes in a review, without the written permission of the publisher.

For information, address:
  The Permanent Press
  4170 Noyac Road
  Sag Harbor, NY 11963
  www.thepermanentpress.com

Library of Congress Cataloging-in-Publication Data

LeClair, Tom.
  Lincoln's Billy / Tom LeClair.
    pages ; cm
  ISBN 978-1-57962-408-8
    I. Title.

PS3562.E2776L56 2015
813'.54—dc23   2014048180

Printed in the United States of America.

For Annaliki Antoniou

O what shall I hang on the chamber walls?
And what shall the pictures be that I hang on the walls,
To adorn the burial-house of him I love?

—WALT WHITMAN,
     "When Lilacs Last in the Dooryard Bloom'd"

PART ONE

CHAPTER ONE

I was Lincoln's Billy. Billy club when Lincoln refused to knock heads in Springfield. Billy goat when he needed a battering ram to reach Washington. Billy boy when he required a charming Billy to scare up money for his campaigns. It was "Lincoln and Herndon" on the shingle hanging outside our office at Sixth and Adams, and our clients called me Mr. Herndon or Herndon. I was "Injin Bill" when a boy roaming fields and forest, "Will" to my friends around town until they took up Lincoln's "Billy." I understood. Lincoln was nine years older when he asked me to partner up with him at the end of 1844. I was twenty-five. I had been studying my Blackstone and Chitty in his office for three years and just passed the bar. With his standing in the capital, Lincoln could have asked just about any experienced lawyer to join him. People who knew us both could not understand why Lincoln chose me. They said he owed my father a political favor or Lincoln felt sorry for his wayward apprentice or calculated I would bring cash into the firm. They did not know what Lincoln said when he made his offer: "Billy, I can trust you, if you can trust me." The first part of that statement was pure Lincoln in its directness, but the second part was odd because Lincoln was already called "Honest Abe" and had a reputation for trustworthiness not universally observed in practitioners of the law. I trusted him.

For twenty years, Lincoln trusted me to hunt down precedents for our cases, trusted me to do the office books and split the cash, trusted me to keep the firm going when he went off to the House of Representatives in 1847 and then the White House. The day before he left in February of 1861, he came by the office to say good-bye.

"Well, Billy, here's my key. Now you won't have to change the lock."

"I didn't think you'd sneak in tonight and steal my Emerson to guide you in the White House."

"No, and you can keep your troublemaking Stowe, too. But now you can find yourself a man to paint over that sign if you want."

"I'm satisfied with it if you are, Mr. Lincoln. Not every lawyer in Springfield is the partner of a president."

"The election of a president don't change the firm of Lincoln and Herndon," he said, lapsing into his Kentucky accent and grammar he liked to use when speaking to me because I, too, was Kentucky born. "If I live, I'm coming back sometime, and then we'll git right to practicing law as if nothing had ever happened."

I remember all those words exactly because I have thought about them every day since April 15, 1865, when James Plumley was pounding on my front door at six in the morning. When I opened up, he stood there looking like he was going to scream "fire" but was too out of breath after his run from the telegraph office. Instead he started sobbing and wheezing. Finally he sobbed out, "The president has been assassinated." And then he asked, "What do you know?" as if Lincoln's Billy standing barefoot in his nightshirt would have some knowledge mysteriously gained during Plumley's dash. Lincoln sometimes joked that I was too long in my briefs, was "willy-nilly with words." But I could not get out a single word to Plumley. I knew nothing, could say nothing. I motioned him into the parlor. As I ran upstairs to tell my wife and to get dressed, Plumley shouted, "Lincoln was shot."

"Assassinated?" Anna asked, not yet fully awake. "Does that mean the president is dead?"

"I don't know. I'm going down to the telegraph office."

Anna was crying now. We were both crying. "As soon as you know . . ."

"Of course, right away."

Plumley and I rushed to the office. Already a dozen people were standing outside. As we came up, they shouted Plumley's question, "What do you know, Billy? What do you know?"

"No more than you," I had to tell them. "That's why I'm here."

Soon the dozen became two dozen and more, all asking Lincoln's partner what he knew. They were fearful and desperate; hard men were crying, tugging their beards, kicking the dirt, cursing the rebels. For some reason, brothers Lawrence and David Johnson were facing each other and slapping each other on the shoulders, like some mourning rite in a primitive land. Old Hugh Spaulding was sitting on the board sidewalk looking dazed, as if he'd been poleaxed.

While we waited for that damned clacking machine to bring us words from Washington, I felt I needed to be Lincoln's surrogate: calm, stoic, a fatalist. But I also wanted to comfort the people who looked to me for news. I was the talker in the office, Lincoln's spokesman during his campaigns, a frequent speaker at civic events. When Lincoln had one of his hypos, he would go still as a scarecrow, silent as a weather vane while he gazed out the window at the people he thought must be fools to be walking the streets, speaking to their friends. Sometimes I could haul him back to life by asking him to tell one of his stories. So even though I was as shocked and afraid as those waiting, I walked among acquaintances and friends and strangers and turned their questions around, asked them how they knew Lincoln, when they last saw the president, what he had said. Lincoln could console people with his presence, as if his homely face and slight stoop and dangling arms spoke the words "I know, I know" to those who suffered. I was just Lincoln's Billy, no gangling giant, only an ordinary man, no stovepipe hat to make me appear taller, just an already grieving lawyer whose work was asking questions.

Some in the crowd blurted out their first contact with Lincoln, as if they needed to begin their own personal biography of the president. Two of our clients mentioned the way he reported judgments for or against them, "Well, I reckon that's settled then." Spaulding struggled to stand up when I approached him and said, "He was standing on the back of that railcar taking him to the White House. We all saw him. You must have been there in the rain that morning, Billy. When war broke out, I knew he'd be coming back laid out." The only woman there, a widow by the name of Earl, said, "I knew Abe as a young 'un up in New Salem. Now hit and Abe are both gone." The Johnson brothers shifted from one boot to another, and Lawrence repeated in a low voice the vulgar joke Lincoln told them about bulls and a lion.

More people joined us, many of them beelining to me. "What do you know, Billy?" I was known as a man quick with words, but this day I was slow and speechless, as if I were the one who had been shot in the head. A few days earlier all the church bells were ringing to celebrate Lee's surrender. Now one bell gonged away as if it knew the news the telegraph would bring. When the clerk stepped out of the office, he was like me, speechless. But the answer to my wife's question was on his face: assassinated meant murdered. The waiting crowd was quiet when he finally read the message. Like the gonging bell, they already knew. Some of my friends came to me to offer their condolences. They shook my hand, they gripped my shoulder, they nodded their heads, but almost no one dared to speak. The occasion was too momentous for words. Abraham Lincoln was often a silent man. The hour he died, Springfield was silent except for that damned bell. Twenty-five years later, I still hear that bell and still have no words to describe the quiet grief of our capital city on that worst day of my long life.

I went home to tell Anna and the children. She could hear the bell and knew.

"No, no, no, William," she said and threw her arms around my neck. "What will you do, what will you do now?"

Again I felt at a loss and could not answer, but I knew even then what I would do is try to keep my partner and friend alive in words. Before Lincoln's death, I had a profession. In the days, weeks, and years to come, I had a vocation. Recite his words, retell his stories.

With my vocation came responsibility. So the next day I dressed in my best black suit and went to the office. Newspapermen from the state and region crowded in, always asking, "What do you know, Billy?" None asked me how I felt. I was just Billy, a possible source. The journalists from out of town wanted to hear new history, something not in Howells's campaign biography: What could I say about Lincoln's early years in Indiana? Was it true Lincoln saved a harmless old Indian's life during the Black Hawk War? Could no man throw him when "wrassling"? Was he attacked by niggers on a trip to New Orleans? What about the rumor that he once fought a duel with James Shields? Did he really jump out a window to prevent a quorum in the legislature? Were you and Lincoln hiding fugitive slaves in your office? From what you know of Lincoln, do you believe he's at God's right hand? Did Lincoln and Herndon send money to John Brown's family? I knew the answers to most of the questions, but that did not mean I was going to give them all away. Like I said before, Lincoln trusted me. He trusted me with money, and he trusted me in party politics. But most of all he trusted me with secrets he told no one else, not his close slaveholding friend Joshua Speed, not his favorite circuit rider Judge David Davis, especially not that unreliable woman he married.

As the journalists kept plucking away at me, I knew there was some information I would not divulge about this person who was my mentor, my partner, my best friend, and the man I loved most in this round world. My father and I quarreled, I had no uncles, my brother was an enemy. At different times in my life, Lincoln was all three relatives to me. He was authority, guide, and confidant. No one else knew Lincoln in all the ways I did. I wanted to make him alive to others as he was to me, so in those first days after his death, long before that interminable funeral train reached Springfield, I started thinking about a "Billy's Lincoln," perhaps a memoir or biography I could write, one containing Lincoln's living speech and vivid stories. After the funeral and after the eulogies that were in every newspaper, I mentioned the idea to my wife.

"You should do it," Anna said. "It will help you through this horror."

After that first day in the office with the reporters, I had not been back. I couldn't bear the reminders. Lincoln had been gone for four years. Now he was gone forever, and yet his desk and books remained. I walked the dirt roads around Springfield. Lincoln hated nature. It would not remind me of my friend.

"Your memories," Anna went on, "would be a comfort to your friends here. His other partners spent nowhere near as much time with him as you. Not even Mrs. Lincoln did."

Speak of horror, I thought, a book by Mary Todd Lincoln.

"Maybe," I said, "but I'm daunted by all the work that would need to be done. This wouldn't be one of those campaign biographies, skimming the surface, skimping the facts. I'm afraid the research would be a huge undertaking."

"Start with what you already know. Give some lectures here in Springfield. You'll get responses from people who also knew Mr. Lincoln, and then you'll know how to go along on a book."

I returned to the office, and recall sitting there, staring at the couch where Lincoln used to lie and read the newspaper, and planning it all out. I will talk to his former partners and other close associates such as James Matheny, the best man at his wedding, and Judge Davis. Follow up my first feeble attempt to console my townsmen with formal interviews. Get outside Springfield, retrace Lincoln's circuit, talk to other lawyers who rode with us. Interview his old acquaintances up in New Salem. Visit the villages in Kentucky and Indiana Lincoln passed through on his way to Illinois. Put our office documents in better order and read back through all the letters he sent me from Washington. Gather documents he wrote from courthouses around the district. Try to talk with Mary Todd, though she took a dislike to me from the first time we met and I complimented her dancing. "Like a serpent," I told her before she was married. I meant her movements were sinuous, but she thought I meant sinful, just the first of her many misunderstandings about the intent of my words.

I once heard Lincoln say that Saul of Tarsus was so drunk he fell off his horse and could not remember his name. I had been knocked off by John Wilkes Booth, and now I had a mission. But not to promote a savior or create a saint. No, from the beginning I felt Billy's Lincoln should be a man with all his qualities displayed, heroic in what he achieved because, given his history, flaws, and quirks, he might have been satisfied to be someone's Billy. Some of that history was well known to others, part of it was known only to me. "What do you know, Billy?" my townsmen asked. I believed it was my responsibility to them and to Lincoln to write what I knew. My purpose was not to convert but to converse, open up a long discussion about our humble man and great president. Lincoln and I were dissimilar in many ways, and we had our differences. Had we been only partners, we would never have lasted all the years we were together. But we were friends, a "tortoise and hare pair," as Lincoln called us, and because we were friends we accepted and often appreciated those differences. Lincoln may even have chosen me for his partner because he wanted some good-natured friction in the office, Old Abe and Young Billy, pessimist and optimist, teller of stories and gatherer of facts. Describing how we differed from each other became part of my mission, a way to get at the enigma Lincoln often was to even his closest friends.

It took only a few days for my mission to put me in trouble. While speaking to members of the bar after the funeral, in the midst of one hundred compliments in my eulogy I mentioned Lincoln was "not as broadminded" as some other men. I meant he was not as broadly read. His former partner, Stephen Logan, rose to contradict and criticize me. It was too early to describe the man, to use any negatives. Lincoln was the Martyr. If Logan, who disagreed with Lincoln on politics, now found him perfect, I assumed the widow would be against my mission, and I predicted that Harvard Robert would want a high-flown portrait of his lowborn father. I should have known that the Republicans who loved the president more when he was dead than when he was alive would oppose my efforts. But I never anticipated I would have to wage my own civil war against a confederacy of secessionists from the truth, fellow citizens from Illinois and Lincoln voters from other states who refused to hear about the Lincoln I knew and the Lincoln I discovered in my research. My own brother, Elliott, another member of the Illinois bar, called me a fool for writing about Lincoln. Anna sometimes doubted the wisdom of my mission. The public conflict began with a lecture I gave in Springfield and dragged on for more than two decades. I was surrounded and besieged, worn down like Lincoln in the White House. Just as Lincoln was betrayed by his generals, I was misled by my potential collaborators. Like Lincoln between 1861 and 1865, I kept losing battles and ground. Over the years, I had to sell off most of my extensive library, my Lincoln "relics" from our office, and much of the land I inherited. But I managed to live long enough to write *Herndon's Lincoln* and, now, this book, which is partly the story of my struggle to write an original biography of an original man.

After devoting many of the last twenty-five years to Lincoln's biography, I decided to compose this brief autobiography, this "Lincoln's Billy," to set the record straight about me—and about Lincoln. *Herndon's Lincoln* was originally going to be *Herndon's Memoirs of Lincoln*, but then the focus shifted toward biography and the memoir elements were left out when the biography was published in 1889. Here I have restored those personal elements about Lincoln and offer a narrative of my life with Lincoln the man and Lincoln the subject. In the biography that Jesse Weik and I prepared, I said that Lincoln was the most secretive man I ever met, so some may question why he would confide the stories here to me. I give some answers to that question, but I have to admit even his confidant does not fully understand why Lincoln seemed to need me to listen. Lincoln was the loneliest married man I ever met. Maybe I was the only person he trusted, like a younger brother or grown nephew. In my research, I found that Lincoln and Joshua Speed had exchanged some revealing but rather general letters about the subject of matrimony, but certain stories about Lincoln's youth he seems to have told only to me, as if I were a biographical depository. These stories were, unfortunately, censored and kept out of *Herndon's Lincoln*.

Over the years, I have been the target of numerous accusations: riding a martyred president's coattails, profiting from a partnership that no longer existed, slandering a president because he did not offer me a government appointment, selling documents he had signed, claiming influence I never had on my partner, making up stories about a man who could not defend himself. Like Lincoln as a young man, I have had, as an older man, my share of faults and failures, but this account is no deathbed confession of wrongdoing. Since the publication of the biography, however, I have been more seriously ill than ever before. At age seventy-one I doubt I have much time left with Anna and my children. I think of this manuscript as my last will and testament and as my family's inheritance, just about the only thing of value I have left to give them. I will direct Anna to see to its publication after my death. Lincoln the man was assassinated. When this manuscript sees print, William Herndon's character will be assassinated. I do have one confession: I lacked the courage to reveal while still alive episodes in Lincoln's life that I recount here. When writing to Weik, I always presented Lincoln in the best possible light. That was what Weik wanted. Now that I no longer depend on a collaborator or fear public enmity, I can put Lincoln—and myself—in noonday light, which may be harsh but true, casting no shadows. Perhaps I will at least be credited with keeping Lincoln's trust and secrets to the grave—his and my own. But as Stanton said when Lincoln passed, "Now he belongs to the ages." *Lincoln's Billy* is for those ages, the truth about our greatest president for Americans in a new century I will not live to see.

PART TWO

Chapter Two

When the journalists who swarmed me after the assassination went home and wrote their eulogies and essays, I was astonished how little truth they contained. Not satisfied with Lincoln's courage and heroism, eloquence and martyrdom, they made him into a prairie demigod or Christian saint. No man I ever met loved truth and understatement more than Lincoln, so I was disgusted on my friend's behalf and angered by the outpouring of slush and sentiment. I wanted to slow the torrent right away before it became a Mississippi of error no man could levee and before it became easy water for Democrats to float their cynical "corrections" on.

Anna and I had been married for three years at that time. From my first suggestion, she had encouraged me to speak about my assassinated partner even though, coming from a Democrat family, she often disagreed with his—and my—politics.

"Start here in Springfield," she said again, advising a lecture or two. "People here know that Mr. Lincoln only looked like some old Biblical figure. Your recollections should be well received."

"By members of your party or by Republicans?"

"By everyone who cares about the truth you'll be able to tell."

"Will the Lincoln lovers trust my truth?"

"The people here will know you loved Lincoln."

Anna was right about that, if not all of my audience. When Lincoln piloted the only steamboat to come down the

Sangamon River almost to Springfield in 1832, I was one of the whooping boys on horseback welcoming the *Talisman.* He was twenty-three and shabby, barefoot on the deck, his pants legs and sleeves all too short. He had no beard then, but his hair looked like a bird's nest on top of his head. His face was dark from his work on rivers, doing some ferrying and piloting. Many years later when riverboat pilot Samuel Clemens became famous as Mark Twain I thought of young Lincoln as the humorous riverman because he picked up stories like passengers wherever he traveled and loved to imitate the accents he heard above and below the old Mason and Dixon line. Back then he surely did not look the man who would guide the ship of state through four years of war. At six feet four inches and sinewy, he appeared better equipped to be a lookout in some low-walled frontier fort. When our welcome party was allowed on board to gawk at its wonders, I remember the tall man was standing near the back of the boat talking to two crew members. They were laughing, and the tall one was looking over the tops of their heads at the folks who had invaded his boat. I wondered then what the odd-looking tall man said to the sailors.

At the time I was thirteen, had my own horse, and had a whole lot more fun in Springfield than Lincoln did as a boy in Kentucky. My friends called me "Injin Bill" because I was a "savage," galloping my horse down muddy streets, tipping over privies, and swimming naked in the Sangamon at night. But my mother was a schoolmarm and gave me more education than Lincoln ever got during his little time in what he called "blab schools." My father was a prosperous business-man, so I also had more prospects than a field laborer, rail-splitter, hog driver, village postmaster, and, to some accounts, a moony layabout. At twenty-one Lincoln left his poor farm-ing family and was trying to support himself doing odd jobs. At the same age, I had spent a year at Illinois College before my father made me return to Springfield because he feared I was becoming an abolitionist. I got a good-paying job in

Joshua Speed's general store, where I spent much of what I earned on shirts and pants that would impress the maidens who came in with their mothers. Working at Speed's, I got the name "Turkey Bill" because, my friends said, I strutted when the girls were about and "gobble gobbled" with anyone who would listen to me. "Gabbled," I told them. Speed's was where I first got to know Lincoln in 1837 when he came to town to be the junior partner of John Todd Stuart. Lincoln looked more like a road-dusted dry goods salesman than a lawyer when he rode in. He was very poor at the time, so he, Speed, Charles Hurst, and I were all sleeping in a room above the store. Lincoln had only a few clothes in a small saddlebag, and they were only a little less shabby than his pilot's gear. He was a lawyer, and I was just a clerk, but I felt sorry for this lonely seeming man down from the hills.

Not long after Lincoln arrived, he kindly asked me why a boy my age was not living with his family, and I learned over time that he also had problems with his father. Thomas Lincoln discouraged his son from studying, worked him hard on land that never satisfied old Thomas, sometimes rented him out to other farmers, and made him stay on the farm until Lincoln reached his majority. The Lincolns moved from state to state, bad land to bad land, and Thomas was never much of a success. Many years later, when Thomas was dying, his son refused to visit him. At the time I roomed with Lincoln, my father had retired from running the Indian Queen Hotel in Springfield and bought himself a farm with the money he made speculating in land. My mother, Rebecca, still taught school so she could, my father said, come into town to buy books. I was the firstborn, and, my brother, Elliott, always said, the fair-haired boy, though my hair was dark like my father's. He was a gregarious man, a local politician who served in the Illinois legislature with Lincoln. When my father was selling drinks in our hotel, he would sit me up on the bar and have me recite doggerel and political slogans. "The poetry was a mistake," Elliott said when we were both studying law. Perhaps he was right because my Jackson Democrat father and I split over politics during my year at college. I'd hoped to be a teacher, but I was pretty happy at the store. Speed paid me well enough to be a fancy dresser for a clerk. I remember I had some patent leather shoes I would take off before I went out in Springfield's dust or mud. I also remember that back then Lincoln had one pair of boots he wore summer and winter and polished, he said, on his birthday.

I believe Lincoln enjoyed rooming with the rest of us at Speed's. We gave him a trapped audience for the stories he loved to tell, tales he'd heard from others, some he made up himself. Down in the store, he and Speed and any customer who had a mind to would huddle around the fireplace in the winter and talk politics. I would join in when I could get away from the cash drawer, but they were older and knew more about local issues. Speed called me "Universal Herndon" because I was more interested in national and international affairs, along with German metaphysics and cosmic mysteries. After the store was closed and we ate our supper, politics gave way to storytelling upstairs, and since many of Lincoln's stories were about "featherbed feelings" a bedroom was the place to hear them. This yarning tradition continued when Lincoln and I and other lawyers were riding the circuit, eating in taverns, and sharing hotel rooms across central Illinois. I did not enjoy the circuit, and up in Speed's dormitory I was no Turkey Bill. I would rather read in quiet than listen to my bunkmates' stories, for the sessions were like minstrel shows, repetitive and predictable. Maybe Lincoln was preparing to be a public speaker with his tales because he'd tell the same story in several different ways, as if he were trying it out for the stage or stump. He was a great admirer of dialect humorists in newspapers, and often got up his stories in their rude manner. He continued this admiration right up into the White House where he read Artemus Ward, Petroleum Nasby, and "Orpheus C. Kerr" to members of the cabinet who were surprised by the crude language because they had not heard Lincoln up in Speed's store.

It is hard to believe, now, that back in those nights Injin Bill was the serious man and melancholy Lincoln was the clown. Or played the role of clown to amuse his friends. After we got familiar, he would ask me what I was reading and, if he thought it foolish, would shout, "Tell us what's in the book, Billy. If ye can't git up a story, read us one." Later I learned that Lincoln also had his nose in books when my age and younger. He taught himself to read from primers and moved on to books about surveying and grammar, but even in the White House a pronunciation from back in Kentucky would sneak through his book "larnin'." When I came back from college, I was reading anything I could find and afford, but my courses got me interested in philosophy along with abolition. Emerson was a favorite but told no stories, so whenever Lincoln asked what I was reading I said *Robinson Crusoe*, the only novel he ever admitted to finishing.

"A great book about pioneer life in America," Lincoln would say, "but I'm mighty surprised you'd be reading such a work, Billy."

"Why do you say that?" I asked the first time, and every other time Lincoln wanted to get off this joke.

"Since you're one of them abolitionists, I figured you'd be strong against Crusoe the slaver keeping himself a boy Friday."

"They became friends."

"That's what's ailing yer damned fiction. Only in a novel about some imaginary island could a white man and a black man be equals."

Several years along, when I was a Friday studying law in Lincoln's office, I was reading scientific works and some poetry. I knew he had written verse as a young man, but when I would read him some lines from William Cullen Bryant or, years later, Whitman, he'd say, "Pipe down, Billy, and listen to this from the *Illinois Journal*." I never met a man more inclined to newspapers, big city or small town, North or South, Democrat or Whig or Republican. From the days when he was learning to read, Lincoln insisted on reciting his newspapers aloud in the office, maybe hoping their facts and lies would drown out my Transcendentalists. When we were partners, he took to declaiming passages from his tragic Shakespeare, all fate and futility, against my Spencer and Darwin, hope and futurity. With his strong memory, Lincoln could hurl about a bunch of lines from the tragedies, but sometimes he would get the Kentuckian mixed in with the Elizabethan and they'd become comedies.

Not long after we entered our partnership I realized I had read a lot more law than Lincoln. I believe he never read a law book cover to cover. We both appeared in court, but he often depended on my research. To other lawyers I was not Lincoln's Billy but "Lincoln's reader." I used to say that in our firm I did the reading and Lincoln did the thinking. Lincoln was like a douser; his wand would dive at the exact place to drill into a case, but he did not share my interest in thinking about thinking. Lincoln was practical and conservative, content with common sense and received wisdom. I was looking for new ways to understand the earth and its inhabitants, and was impatient with inherited social conventions. Lincoln wanted the statutory law from the past that governed a particular case; "Universal Herndon" searched for the scientific law that would govern all cases in the future.

If Lincoln's autobiography is any indication, were he writing my biography, it would be a collection of facts about my Whig background, my contributions to our new Republican Party, my labors on his and others' campaigns—and then my mysterious departure from politics to farm and read and write. After his years in the Illinois House, Lincoln was a politician top to bottom, even when he was not running for or holding office. He had little interest in the psychology of an individual, only in the mind of the majority, whether voters on a jury or at the polls. As a young man, I was active in party politics and helped Lincoln in many a canvass, activities I covered in detail in the biography. I was even elected mayor of Springfield for a year, but I never thought of myself as a politician. You needed to be one to become president, of course, but what I wanted to be was the man—the force— that moved politicians, that modified their minds and directed their actions with my writing. While arguing five-dollar cases about property lines at Lincoln and Herndon in the fifties, I started writing for newspapers and corresponding with men I considered the intellectual lights of my generation: Emerson, Theodore Parker, William Lloyd Garrison, and others. Late now in this century, their influence has faded, but before the war they were the advanced guard. Some would even say they were the skirmishers who instigated the war that Lincoln resisted as long as he could. He famously told Harriet Beecher Stowe that she was the "little lady" who started the war. I doubt Lincoln read her novel, but I did and, I have to admit, envied her force, even if it was through fiction.

Lincoln thought novels were a waste of paper, ink, and time. "Low lying," he said one day when he saw me reading Cooper's *The Prairie*.

"Under water for millions of years," I said.

"I mean the author."

"Like your Shakespeare?"

"Ah, that's high lying about history."

"Low lying like Stowe's might be necessary in a desperate present."

"You git to feeling matters is desperate, Billy, I'll read your novel if you write it up in verse."

Although Lincoln could quote long passages from Byron and Burns, he would not listen to me read Emerson. Lincoln had heard the sage of Concord lecture in Springfield, but I was pretty sure Lincoln never read his essays. Still, if he heard me talking about Emerson with one of the boys studying with us, Lincoln would throw down a comment to get a rise out of me. He hated to prepare a case but loved the give and take of the courtroom, so when he could he would turn our little office into a debating chamber. He preferred an audience, but if I were the only one around Lincoln would see what agitation he could drum up between us. I do not pretend to remember exactly, but our conversations would go something like this:

"I do understand that self-reliance, Billy, because that's who I relied on when driving hogs up in New Salem. When they wouldn't board our flatboat to see the sights of New Orleans, me and Offutt sewed their eyes shut. We got along pretty straight after that. So I don't understand this 'transparent eyeball.'"

"That's because your eyeball sees the world as a bunch of hogs to be driven, Mr. Lincoln. The transparent eyeball gives you intuition, unclouded insight into the profound inner workings of other men and nature."

I'd get out my copy of "Nature" and try to read him some lines, but he would wave them off.

"I reckon I pretty much know what I need to about the innards of nature from helping butcher them hogs."

"Emerson says we betray our new and better selves if we look only at what we can butcher."

"Shoot, Billy, I know that. That's why I use my other eyeball to observe the doings of our better brethren, them bipeds who walk through that door over thar and hire me and you to help them cheat some neighbor out of property or jimmy some family member out of their inheritance. Sometimes they give me a hypo."

"That's why you should read Emerson. He'd turn your hypo into hope. He's optimistic about improving the race, improving each individual, improving the social conditions that make men into plaintiffs and defendants."

"That sounds just about perfect, Billy, but with too much improvement, you and me'd be full out of business. Which reminds me of a businessman named Perry who owned a hardware store down in Egypt. He tried to improve the conditions of the village streets by arguing for an ordinance against horseshit. Well, not agin it, exactly, but requiring each owner of a horse or team to pick up his horses' shit. Turned out Perry had invented some manner of scoop you could use while in the saddle for just that purpose. The ordinance never passed but Perry got himself a new name. You've heard of 'shit-kicker,' right? Waal, people down thar forever after called him 'shit-picker Perry.'"

The law students that I supervised would shoot questioning looks to me. I was never certain when Lincoln was serious, half-serious, or joking, but we heard the shit-picker story many times. In my assigned and enjoyed role back then as Lincoln's interlocutor—the earnest neophyte and prim voice of Eastern refinement to his crafty vulgarian—I would never say to Lincoln that, compared to the great-souled Emerson, he was the shit-picker, always taking or pretending to take the low road when high ideals were introduced into a conversation. When discussing law or justice before the court, Lincoln was like an ideal judge, carefully examining every side of a matter. Debating against Douglas or speaking at Cooper Union, Lincoln was the idealistic politician, eloquently calling Americans to their better selves. But in the office or out on the circuit he was a mighty Kentucky-bred scoffer. One of his older friends, Matheny I believe it was, told Lincoln he was "two-faced," and Lincoln said, "If you had a face like mine, you'd want a second one." I could not retell his oft-told and off-color stories in my lectures or biography, but any man who talked very long with Lincoln would hear a story like the one about Perry. Lincoln once said his stories stunk "like a thousand privies," but that was inaccurate for about five hundred smelled of sweaty featherbeds. Fortunately, we had few ladies as clients in those days. If we did, we would have needed to clean up Lincoln's language and the office, where once we found weeds growing out of dirt in a corner.

In the courtroom, Lincoln sometimes played the role of bumpkin. I, too, tucked my pants into my boots, chewed on a sliver, and said "damn" and "hell," but our method was completely different. I was still Turkey Bill gobbling over every word and issue as I tried to wear down opposing attorneys and witnesses. I could quote reams of case law, and had no problem working myself up to long impassioned summations because my engine always seemed to run faster and hotter than my partner's. Laconic Lincoln lounged about the court-room as if it were a stable, sat on the table, dug earwax out of his ears, and used anecdotes to illustrate the arguments his powerful analytic mind measured out. I was good with judges. He was a master at influencing a jury after keeping one eye on them during a trial, but when we had to do a hurry-up voir dire Lincoln trusted my swift impressions. He would laugh and say, "You pick 'em, Billy, with your transparent eyeball."

Most of our clients were farmers, and we were surely country lawyers with plenty of time to talk until our crops came in. When Lincoln wasn't away on the circuit or out politicking, he and I discussed all manners of things, from cases and clients to science and Shakespeare. He helped me see through complications, I helped him see complications. If he needed to be alone in the office, I would vacate. If I needed a little extra cash, he would advance some of his share. It is difficult to trace, now, how a mentorship and partnership became a friendship. Perhaps the answer is simple: a long time in a short space, a familiarity that bred respect rather than contempt. We were so accustomed to each other's presence that when we passed each other in the street we often did not acknowledge our partner. We tolerated each other's irritating habits—my spitting tobacco juice, his snoring on his couch in the afternoon—because we shared a fundamental dedication to justice. We may have come to the law with different motives, but over the years it was justice that kept us in the law—and eventually led Lincoln to seek the presidency. And, I suppose, led me to write this book doing justice to my partner and best friend.

CHAPTER THREE

When writing up my first lecture, I wanted to dam the slush, but I did not want my discussion of Lincoln to depend on just our friendship and my personal knowledge, even though they went back more than two decades. As if I were preparing a case for Lincoln, I decided to do some preliminary research, investigate what those who knew him before I did had to say about the development of his character, my lecture topic. I interviewed John Todd Stuart, his former law partner; N. W. Edwards, Mary Todd's brother-in-law; James Gurley, who lived next door to the Lincolns; and many others in Springfield. I went to eastern Illinois to interview Lincoln's aged stepmother, and I traveled to Gentryville, Indiana, to see the Lincolns' old farm and speak with people who remembered Abraham as a boy. I conferred with John Hanks, Lincoln's cousin, who was the only person who claimed to know anything about Lincoln's two trips as a young man to New Orleans, trips that Lincoln believed greatly influenced his ambition to become a city man rather than a dirt man or riverman, to live comfortable instead of raw, to be worthy of a woman like the Lexington-raised Mary Todd. Hanks gave me a long written statement in which he said he accompanied Lincoln to New Orleans where he developed his disgust with slavery. Later I found out Hanks went only as far south as Saint Louis. Not all informants, not even relatives, could be believed, so on the subject of New Orleans I trusted Lincoln's own stories.

Although Lincoln had little to say about his family and his poverty before he came to Springfield, when his mood was strong and business was slow he would talk to me about river life and big city life in tones I rarely heard in his voice, wonder at his adventurous younger self and nostalgia for a locale that made Springfield seem like one of the hamlets he passed through on the way here. Because Lincoln most enjoyed retelling stories with comic endings, I heard the following many times in the early years of our partnership and can at some points quote him exactly and imitate the Kentucky accent he put on to amuse me. I include the whole episode here because it is new biographical information and because Lincoln's experiences in New Orleans came to be crucial to his personal and political life. At appropriate points throughout this book, I retell Lincoln's other New Orleans recollections in, for the most part, chronological order, so they form a single story about the formation of young Abraham's character. "In the heat of New Orleans," he used to say, "I was like the Bible's Abram in the fire."

Lincoln was nineteen when he made his first trip in 1828, working a flatboat's foremost steering oar for his young friend Allen Gentry, who was taking ham and hominy south to sell for his father. Lincoln the expert axman and Gentry built their own flatboat, essentially a large raft with half a roof on it, difficult to maneuver but they would sell the wood along with the cargo in New Orleans. They went in the spring when the water was high and fast. "That Ohio was no Sangamon trickle," Lincoln would say, "but when the Ohio hit the Mississippi them confused currents spun us around like a dog chasing his tail. I never seen a natural danger like that." As was his wont, Lincoln would stretch out the month-long trip downstream, listing the towns they passed, describing the Natchez lighthouse, remarking on the different kinds of estates they saw from cotton country down to sugar plantations. Eventually he would float along to the human danger. About sixty miles below Baton Rouge, he and Gentry tied up to the shore for the night and were attacked by seven Negroes. "I believe they were fugitive slaves desperate for food," Lincoln would say. "Two of them clambered onto the boat. There weren't no wrasslin' to be done with these boys because they were holding clubs. One of them gave me a pretty good swipe on my right ear, but I kept my feet and Gentry hollered, 'Get the guns Lincoln and shoot the niggers.' We didn't have no guns, but that threat scured 'em off. I reckon that shows a lie can work wonders." Then Lincoln would hesitate and say, "We was damned lucky them Africans had been taught English," which was followed by his high, reedy laugh.

In New Orleans, flatboats had their own wharves, a bit up-river from where the steamboats left and farther removed from where the grand coastal ships docked, brigs and schooners bound for or just in from New York, Liverpool, and Le Havre. There were about fifty flatboats tied up, Lincoln said, when they arrived, and nobody was standing on the levee to welcome two "Kaintucks," the name most New Orleans residents called flatboaters, no matter where they came from. Experienced flatboaters' cargo was bought in advance by wholesalers, but Gentry and Lincoln were amateur retailers on their own. "If we hoped to get that pork off our boat, we had to jump up and holler louder than our competition. I was a head taller than anyone, so I could attract some attention. I stood on a box, stretched my arm up above my head, waved my cap, and shouted 'high, high, high quality.' Then I bent down, waved my cap over Gentry who was crouching like one of them organ grinder's monkeys, and hollered 'low, low prices.' I expect it was my first speech to people I didn't know. Soon enough we was known as the 'high-low' boys. There was a lot of cursing and jesting and insulting on that wharf, so we was also known as 'sly and slow.' But we sold off our cargo in two days. I don't remember exactly how much we got, but it was to Gentry's satisfaction."

When they were breaking apart their flatboat, they were approached by several wood buyers bidding on the planks and boards. A man dressed all in white, who Lincoln thought was about forty, came by, surveyed the pile the boys had, and said to Lincoln, "Ye are a natural born 'Kaintuck,' ain't you?" "Well, yes I am but how did you know?" "I heard you talking, and I hail from Paducah myself." The quick-thinking Gentry puts in, "Then you know how fine this Kentucky oak and ash and poplar is, cut not two months ago by the very 'Kaintucks' you see before you." The man looked over what they had and offered a price. Gentry said, "A Hoosier offered us more than that an hour ago." "Ye'll probably get even more from a Sucker," the man replied, using a term then referring to people from Illinois. Lincoln, Gentry, and the man, whose name was James Raymond, all laughed and eventually struck a deal.

Raymond suggested the "sailors" find lodging with Old Mother Colby at the Sure Enuf Hotel in "The Swamp," the neighborhood near the Girod Street Cemetery where most of the flatboaters rented cheap rooms and sampled the lower pleasures of the city—the bars, gambling houses, and brothels. For the next week, Raymond showed his up-country cousins around New Orleans when he had time, mostly at night. They saw four-story buildings for the first time, paved streets with lamplights, many shops in Fauborg Street selling goods Lincoln said they couldn't identify, restaurants serving food they had never seen and were afraid to try. They heard French, Spanish, Creole—Raymond told them—along with other tongues not even he, who had lived in New Orleans for twenty years, could identify. "And newspapers, Billy, you should see all the newspapers hanging up like fresh fish, today's news today, not three weeks late. Bookstores everywhere, if you could afford them. Two theyaters I passed but didn't go in, not dressed in flatboat togs." Lincoln's father was cheated one time when he went south with a flatboat, so Lincoln was at first suspicious of this man who was friendlier than his own father, but he said, "Gentry was holding all the money, so I had no cause to worry over much." After

Raymond took them to his own home, a cottage on Cabildo Street, and had his Negro cook prepare them a gumbo, Lincoln's suspicion of Raymond diminished.

"Any man could see the money thar in New Orleans, Billy. It was passing hands on the docks, walking down the street in polished boots, riding in gold-painted carriages, but I reckon it was that man Raymond who most influenced me. He'd come down from Paducah on a flatboat, as green as me and Gentry. He'd stayed, worked on the docks, lived cheap, put the money he earned with the flatboat money, calculated a way to sell small batches of prime wood, bought careful, built up his business, bought his little house, and had two servants, one to shop and cook, one to clean and launder them white pants and shirts he always wore. And listen, he couldn't cipher any better than me, and I suspect he couldn't read much more than the signs on shops. Yes sir, that Raymond in his white cottons showed me I wouldn't need to chop trees and live in a damned log cabin forever if I could figure some way to git up on a box and use my Kaintucky-born wits."

The first time Lincoln told me about Raymond, I asked if he had a wife to watch over the servants.

"Not that we ever saw or heard about. I reckon Raymond didn't require a wife like you and me. Raymond treated that mulatto cook very friendly-like, and she warn't no weather-beaten field hand, I can tell you that. He also pointed out taverns where a man could git his urges satisfied without paying a preacher."

"How did you know those women were servants and not slaves?"

"I can't rightly know, but Raymond said they were free blacks, and he called the cook Mrs. Caroline."

"But not Mrs. Raymond."

"Not even down thar in New Orleans, Billy."

Raymond knew the best steamboat to take back upriver and when *The Amazon* was leaving. This was before Lincoln was piloting on the Sangamon and was another first for him. It was a two-week trip, and Raymond warned them, as Gentry's father had, to be on the lookout for sharpers who rode the boats trying to relieve Kaintucks of their New Orleans cash. Gentry was so nervous about pickpockets or other thieves, he asked Lincoln to carry a share. "He trusted me with half, Billy, just like I trust you. But a funny thing happened one night when I went to the bar with Gentry. Behind the bar I spotted a small sign that read 'No Trust.' I pointed it out to Gentry. He tapped my right front pants pocket where I kept my half and said, 'I hope that's the money and not your steering oar, Abe.' 'Since I ain't a Christian,' I told him, 'I keep my oar over by my left pocket. You can feel it yourself if you don't trust me.'"

Again that high whinny laugh of Lincoln's. Even if you did not think a story was all that funny the second or third time around, Lincoln could start you to laughing at the sight and sound of him laughing. He was a different man when telling a story, and I suppose that is why he would drop anything if one occurred to him. It always seemed a pity to me that Lincoln's stories were left out of biographies, including my own, for they often revealed, if only indirectly, the man Lincoln otherwise kept secret.

CHAPTER FOUR

Most of the interviews I did before my first lecture, while useful for a full historical portrait, just gave me the kind of facts a conventional biographer would use to record what Lincoln did and said. If I had been a newspaper reporter, I might have been satisfied with the anecdotes I collected. I wanted to describe the man, but more importantly I wanted to analyze the qualities of character familiar to me that eventually made him an excellent trial lawyer and a great statesman. I had read George Herbert Spencer's *Principles of Psychology* not long after it was published in 1855 and was much drawn to Spencer's scientific approach to mind and thus to character. Spencer studied how consciousness in lower organisms responded to their environment and how they evolved into human consciousness that was also partly defined by its environment. From the first years knowing Lincoln, I sensed that he was a distinctive "organism," that his early natural environment and certain qualities of his physiology and even his physiognomy greatly influenced his psychology. In my lectures, I wanted to do for Lincoln what Spencer did for humans in general: provide a naturalistic and profound analysis of how different traits combine to form a complex individual. Emerson was fine for inspiring individual intuition, but I needed a more scientific basis for my lectures on Lincoln's mind if they were going to counter the myths that were already making him more than human and, in my opinion, less a human like the rest of us.

Lincoln in his youth had been an athlete, capable of impressive feats of running, lifting, weight tossing, and wrestling. Though I never saw him wrestle or play town ball, now known as base ball, I several times played him at "fives" or handball. We struck against the solid wall of the Presbyterian church and agreed the building was good for something. Although older and seemingly awkward, Lincoln was very nimble, had tremendous reach, and powerful leverage with his long arms. He always beat me easily and never conceded a point. He used to say I spent too much time in the soft featherbed and not enough time on the hard circuit. Against that church wall, I recognized Spencer's "survival of the fittest" in Lincoln the organism. It was from his able body that he drew his strong will and desire to win, both of which served him well through his trials during the war.

My first two lectures in December of 1865 were sponsored by the Business College of Rutledge and Davidson in Springfield. As Anna predicted, they were well attended. I had been speaking in behalf of Lincoln as a candidate for many years, but analyzing his character was different, and I was nervous at this beginning of my "mission." I began, as Spencer would, with Lincoln's perceptions of the world, which I said were "cold, clear, and exact," perhaps because of the "low and feeble circulation of his blood" or his slow responses "to the effects of stimuli." I then discussed how he associated ideas but insisted on the "causative," on understanding the origin of a sensation or idea. Because, as I said at the time, "He had a wider and deeper comprehension of his environments than men who were more learned," his mind was like a "majestic machine running in deep iron grooves with heavy flanges on its wheels." It was this mechanism of truth, not inherited faith of any kind, from which Lincoln's strong conscience developed. When that mind judged what was true and just, Lincoln could not be shaken by petty devices. A lesser man—a less unique organism—would have collapsed under the pressures exerted by the Washington environment. And it was only when Lincoln found Grant, an organism as relentless as the president, that Lincoln was able to win the war.

I had much more to say about other positive qualities of Lincoln's character, but I believe the Spencerian orientation suggested by these samples contributed most to the effect of the lectures. My brother, Elliott, demonstrated the dated kind of analysis that my new science displaced. He wrote a note to me saying that "physiologically and phrenologically Lincoln was a sort of monstrosity . . . The man's mind partook of the incongruities of his body." Like many at midcentury, Elliott was still stuck on the shape of a person's head rather than the shape of his brain or experience. Later I explained Lincoln's odd "double consciousness," his sudden shifts from gloom to geniality and back, as a product of his "double brain": "one life in one hemisphere of the brain and the other life in the other." When I saw Elliott at the courthouse one day, he said, "Let him go. You make a greater fool of yourself lecturing about this dead man than when you were writing his campaign speeches." I said only, "Have you never noticed my sagacity bump, brother Elliott?"

Lincoln's close friends Leonard Swett and Senator Lyman Trumbull praised my lectures. Many newspapers around the nation carried positive stories about them, and a man from Baltimore named Francis Carpenter used, without my permission, material from the lectures for his *Six Months at the White House*, a very popular book from which I saw no earnings. Though not legal, this was a precedent for others who wrote about Lincoln, just one form of the piracy I suffered for decades. The lectures also attracted the attention of a young law student in Philadelphia, Charles Henry Hart, who was compiling a bibliography of items about Lincoln. After a lengthy correspondence, we discussed collaborating on a book, and Ticknor and Fields—which published Emerson!—was very interested in bringing out our combination of biography and bibliography.

Then came Josiah Holland's *Life of Abraham Lincoln*. It sold one hundred thousand copies, took the wind out of the Herndon and Hart sails, angered me with its presentation of Lincoln as a Christian, and initiated this science-influenced biographer's long war with religion-based hagiographers. While an editor of the *Springfield Republican* in Massachusetts, Holland had come all the way to Illinois in the spring of 1865 to ask me about Lincoln. Holland was a failed doctor but successful novelist who knew popular tastes. His high sloping forehead and flowing mustache made him appear to be a man who put his face into the winds of the future, but one of his first questions indicated the direction of his interests: "What about Mr. Lincoln's religion?"

"The less said the better," I told him.

"Why do you say that?"

"Because Lincoln was a skeptic from his youth and for all the years I knew him. It's still too early to put before the public everything about this subject."

"Oh never mind," Holland said, "I'll fix that."

"You may ignore it, as I did in my lecture when I crossed out some planned comments. But trust me on this, there is no fixing the facts, the reports I have collected and remarks I have heard from Lincoln's own mouth."

"One has only to read Lincoln's speeches with their quotations from the Old and New Testaments to recognize the essential Christianity of the man."

"Lincoln read and reread the Bible when young because it was one of the few books he could get. He also read Aesop's *Fables*. He used both for illustrating principles, but I assure you that Lincoln was a man of no faith, except in his own perceptions and mind."

Holland had the believer's response to my empirical arguments: "I refuse to believe what you say about our nineteenth-century savior." I kept my temper. I did not contend with this godly fool. But after this comment, there was no reason to tell Holland what he could have known from some basic

investigation in Illinois. In his biography, Holland the journal-
ist was overcome by Holland the pious man and Holland the
novelist who "fixed" the religious issue with fabrications that
would please his readers:

"Sad and weary, working early and late, full of the
consciousness that God was working through him for the
accomplishment of great ends, praying daily for strength and
guidance, with a heart full of warm charity toward his foes,
and open with sympathy toward the poor and the suffering, this Christian President sat humbly in his high seat, and
did his duty . . . Moderate, frank, truthful, gentle, forgiving,
loving, just, Mr. Lincoln will always be remembered as emi-
nently a Christian President; and the almost immeasurably
great results which he had the privilege of achieving, were
due to the fact that he was a Christian President."

The hypocrisy of this Christian lying in print infuriated
me. I wanted to respond immediately, announce a lecture
on Lincoln's "religion" or put out a broadside, but Anna said
I should save my reply for my biography, perhaps because
on religion we did not see transparent eye to eye. Although
Anna the Democrat was not opposed to slavery when we
first met, I managed to persuade her after many "torture" sessions to my way of thinking on the race issue. In later years
she even became fond of William Lloyd Garrison, who visited
us in Illinois. But Anna was also raised a Presbyterian, and
no amount of Spencer or Whitman or Herndon could dis-
turb her faith in Christian salvation and damnation. I put my
faith in Emerson's "Divinity School Address," with its denial
of the Biblical God and its intuition of the spirit all around.
Lincoln was a Tom Paine man. For Lincoln, God was far
removed, the old Deists' machinist, but even that he scoffed
at. "Clockmaker? Cockmaker is how we all got here," he
would say. For me, the spiritual was closer but no more
personal.

Anna would say to me, "It's a good thing you're a good
man, William, because if salvation was truly by faith alone

you'd be spending eternity in hell listening to Lincoln retell his stories forever."

"No, no, Anna. I have no fear of that afterlife. What I would fear, if I believed, would be ending up in the same place as that believer Mary Todd. She could make even heaven a hell for those she disliked."

My informants who knew Lincoln before he came to Springfield and needed to ingratiate himself as lawyer and politician told me that he used to entertain customers at Offutt's store in New Salem with parodies of the local preachers and mockeries of the inconsistencies and absurdities he found in his reading of the Bible. He even went so far as to write an exposition of Infidelism, which was there and then the popular term for religious skepticism. Lincoln planned to publish this essay as a pamphlet, but his friend Samuel Hill was so offended that he tossed the manuscript into the fire, which was a real loss for biographers such as Holland. In Springfield, Lincoln debated religious issues with our mutual friend Albert Bledsoe who said Lincoln "always seemed to deplore his want of faith as a very great infelicity." I mention these witnesses because I know that some among the faithful will even now refuse to believe me when I say that Lincoln told me many times that he did not believe that the Bible contained the revelations of a God monitoring and, in his word, "fingering" human affairs.

Despite Lincoln's disbelief, he was superstitious, and it bothered him because he could not understand why. Spencer would say it was the residue of his youth in an environment where adults believed that a dog crossing a hunter's path was bad luck unless the hunter locked his little fingers together.

"My father," Lincoln told me once, "would never plant on Fridays because it was bad luck, and potatoes had to be planted at night because they grew underground, in the dark."

"You believed him?"

"I didn't know. I was just a child. My mother used to tell me that if I brought my ax into the cabin it would bring a death within a year."

"Did it ever happen?"

"I'm not certain about that. After she died when I was nine, I tried hard to remember if I'd brought an ax into the house."

Lincoln looked away from me and shook his head, as if he were trying to dismiss some long-held guilt. What could I say? I told Lincoln he was just a boy then, that I always brought my ax into the house. But the conversation ended.

On another occasion, Lincoln told me about going to a voodoo fortune-teller down in New Orleans, probably because he knew this "confession" would amuse me.

"You don't believe in any religion," I told him, "but you thought a voodoo priest could predict your future?"

"Waal, I believe it was a priestess, so black she was almost blue, but her body was all swaddled up in robes and belts and beads. I could hardly tell if she was a woman or a man."

"Did you see men in robes and beads?"

"This was New Orleans, Billy. You can see most anything down thar. Me and Gentry saw a man draped in a sheet lugging a wooden cross around the streets and hollering the end were near. I mighta thought it was Jesus come round for a second try except he had good lace-up boots on and no holes in his hands I could see. Gentry hollered at him, 'Which end?' and the feller pulled up his sheet and showed us his ass."

"I guess it wasn't Jesus then."

"No, and come to think of it Jesus wouldn't have been speaking English, though one of the shouters up in New Salem said he could speak in all tongues. Reverend Smythe said that's why the French and Italians and such call themselves Christians. Because Jesus could speak their lingo as well as he could English."

"What about the fortune-teller, what did she tell you?"

"Not much. I think Raymond put me in with her as a joke. I don't reckon she knew as much English as Jesus."

"Well, what did she say?"

" 'Something wicked this way comes,' " Lincoln said, starting to laugh before he could finish.

Lincoln was pulling on my leg but also giving me a little Shakespeare reading test.

"So that priestess was a witch, was she?"

"Actually, Billy, she said, 'You will have big cock.' "

Somehow Lincoln kept a straight face this time.

"I'm supposed to believe that?"

"I swear, that's what she said. I believe Raymond put her up to it because she laughed loud and long as she collected my fifty cents."

"Maybe knowing how tall you were, she made a logical and scientific prediction. Or a lucky guess."

"I don't know, Billy. Do you reckon thirteen inches is an unlucky number?"

Lincoln probably made up his dialogue with the fortune-teller to amuse me, but he did admit to visiting one. Spencer would attribute Lincoln's folly to his environment and the magical thinking that preceded logical thinking based on perceptions and "causative" analysis. When I told Lincoln this, he said, "Bring that Spencer feller to Springfield. Maybe he can persuade me that the bird that got into our house this morning ain't bad luck. And if he can't, he can help me catch it because I can't kill it." Lincoln could be a very tenderhearted man, one reason so many people who barely knew him loved him as "Father Abraham." For many years, that was the Lincoln I knew, admired, and loved, but I also knew that my friend could be a hard man. He had to be to send thousands to their deaths in the war. That was the thesis of my third lecture, in January of 1866, on Lincoln's statesmanship.

CHAPTER FIVE

Herbert Spencer could take me far into the mine shaft—the mind shaft—of Lincoln's psychology, but not all the way down to the dark space of his hypos, those depressions of spirit that afflicted him, periods of melancholy that defied his powers of analysis and caused his friends to speculate on their origin. Anyone could understand his and his wife's extended mourning for their beloved boy Willie, who died in the White House, or the infant child they lost while still in Springfield. I understood the periodic and usually passing sadnesses caused by his dust-ups with Mary Todd, and I knew that what other people saw as melancholia in Lincoln's silences and brown studies was sometimes merely his mind working over some problem that interested him. But what I most wanted to analyze and explain to others—without betraying any of Lincoln's secrets—in my fourth Springfield lecture was why Lincoln once told a friend he had "run off the track" and told another friend he had been so overcome with the hypos that he "dared not carry a knife in his pocket" for fear of what he would do to himself. On these two occasions, friends felt he was a danger to himself and watched him closely.

Although Lincoln's mind was an efficient, lucid machine, his heart had a vast capacity for sympathy both personal and general. It was one of his finest traits, people sensed this, and I benefitted from it. But the strange truth is he lacked intuition, not just Emerson's piercing insight but everyday awareness of people unlike him, by which I mean everybody but primarily women and, more specifically, the women he courted. One of them, Mary Owens, described that failure of feeling or sensitivity as a want of "those little links that would make up the great chain of woman's happiness." This deficiency of intuition caused Lincoln no end of troubles with women. I could not describe these intimate troubles in a lecture so soon after his death—not even in my biography almost three decades after his death—but I can reveal here some of the domestic problems that contributed to Lincoln's melancholia.

I long wondered about this difference in intuition between us and could explain it only by our early upbringing. Life in a log cabin on an isolated farm did not require much subtle feeling for others. Spending much of my youth in my father's hotel, taking drink orders, and running errands for guests, I developed, I believe, the ability to intuit others' feelings and minds and characters. When working at Speed's store, I practiced anticipating what customers would ask for. I read books and I read faces. I called this ability my "mud instinct." Lincoln seemed to me to labor at understanding or sympathizing with other people. Lacking an immediate sense of others, he ran them through his logic and judged them. I think that's why he seemed so lethargic. He was thinking about how he should feel about the person in front of him.

The women he courted before the well-born and refined Mary Todd came from families more successful than Lincoln's, which was not difficult considering his father could not read and discouraged Lincoln from learning how. When Mary Todd came up from Kentucky to visit her sister in Springfield, she was practically a touring aristocrat, one who could speak French from her days in a private academy for women. She was kind of a bitty woman, but she knew how to dress so her plump chest was shown off to advantage when men looked down at her, and she knew how to flirt with any man who did not use a cane. And, as I have said, she knew how to dance. After a few months of awkward courtship, Lincoln proposed to her, changed his mind, told her he did not love her, and then after almost two years had passed married her in a rush in November 1842. It was a strange "lash-up," as Lincoln might say. The two groomsmen were given a few hours notice, and Mary Todd's sister had no time to bake a cake.

Nobody around Springfield understood why Lincoln would go back and marry a woman he had betrayed, especially one as proud and hot-tempered as Mary Todd. That decision was surely a failure of intuition, or maybe the sacrifice of intuition to honor. Lincoln's first law partner, John Stuart, called the union a "policy match all around," which meant Lincoln would get himself refined and Mary Todd would get herself a promising husband. On his wedding day, Lincoln was asked where he was going all dressed up, and he answered, "To hell, I guess." When the Lincolns' first child was born close to nine months after the marriage date, gossips in town said it was a hell of Lincoln's own making. Or, more likely, Mary Todd's. Lincoln liked to joke about men hornswoggled into weddings, but I never heard him or anyone in his hearing joke about Mary Todd inviting him to lift her skirts. One of Lincoln's favorite riddles was: "How is a woman like a barrel?" The answer was, "You have to raise the hoops before you put the head in." Whatever head impelled him to enter marriage with Mary Todd, he never got himself out of it. She wore herself and Lincoln out trying to improve him, but at least he got an improved house from the match. When he was out on the circuit for a long stay, Mary used some money from her father to add rooms to their house. Lincoln used to joke that he came back and asked someone on his street where Abe Lincoln lived. But it was only half a joke because much of the time he lived on the road and some of the time at the office.

If Mary was in one of her moods when Lincoln got home from the office, she would make it hot around the house and back he would come to the office, sometimes sleeping on the extra long couch he bought. Neighbors around Eighth and Jackson could hear her curse like a drover. Some mornings she chased him out with a broomstick because he was not properly attending to his chores, and he would come early to the office, sit on his sofa, and have a dry breakfast. On those occasions, he would never say anything about his Mary but would sometimes ask about my Mary, as if comparing our domestic situations. That was my beloved first wife, Mary Maxcy. Maybe because of my father's success running his hotel and then speculating in land, I did not need to marry up. Sideways was fine after I fell in love with Mary when I was twenty-two and she was eighteen. She used to come in Speed's, and I would ask her if she wanted more of the miracle compound that made her hair blonde. She was a very modest girl for someone so pretty. When I first asked her to meet me for a walk after work, she said, "Do you know who my father is?" "Marshal Maxcy, I believe." "Yes, and he thinks all young men are up to no good." I had better luck after I saw her at a meeting organized by some visiting abolitionists.

"Is your father present?" I asked her.

"Not that I can see," she said.

"There could be trouble tonight with these folks. If there is, you just hold on to my coat, and I'll take care of you."

"But that coat is orange," she said, wide-eyed and smiling.

"Top of the line at Speed's, imported from France by way of the finest clothier in New York City. All the chevaliers in Paris and the smart folks in Manhattan are wearing this coat. Do you read French? If so I could show you the label, though it might be improper to unbutton my coat for a lady in public. I put it on tonight because I thought you might be here, and I wanted you to be able to find me if a fight breaks out."

As I said, I was a gobbler back in my youth. After that night listening to the abolitionists with their strange Massachusetts accents, Mary and I would talk about politics at the store. She was a smart girl and not at all frivolous in her purchases, so, after finding out if she could cook, I trusted my intuition, asked Marshal Maxcy for his daughter's hand, and was rewarded with a wife who called me "sweet William."

We saw through the same transparent eyeball. Although she didn't have my schooling, she read books I had no time for and wrote up digests of them for me. She also read the magazines I brought home. One of her favorite writers was Edgar Allan Poe, and she joked during Lincoln's campaigns that I was his "William Wilson," his conscience. Two William Wilsons and two Marys. My Mary and Lincoln's Mary couldn't have been more different, so I called my wife "Marymax." Like me, she wished Lincoln was more aggressive against slavery and had read the books that argued for its abolition.

Lincoln used to say that I was way ahead of him in the production of heirs, for we had four by the time his first son was born. Maybe because I was young, the children were like playmates. I was continually pulling pranks on them, and I enjoyed being around them. A late father, Lincoln loved his children but often was abstracted or inattentive when they were about. Marymax called me "professor" at home. In the winter, when the children came home from school I would drill them on their arithmetic and grammar. In the summer I used to take them out into the fields and woods and teach them what I knew of geology and botany. Lincoln should have come with us. Instead he brought his Willie and Tad to the office and let them run wild as if they were out of doors. Lincoln may have once herded hogs, but not his boys. After a few hours chasing them around, trying to save our furniture and files, I would go home and complain to Marymax. She and anyone who lived within range of Mary Todd's voice knew about Lincoln's problems with her, and Marymax's woman's intuition helped me understand the boys and Lincoln.

"Lincoln refuses to control them," I told her after a day in which they broke two pens. "They have no discipline."

"Wasn't Mr. Lincoln severely disciplined as a boy by his father?"

"I believe so. But that's no excuse."

"And didn't he have a gentle stepmother who moderated the father?"

"Yes, but I don't see the point."

"Didn't you tell me you thought that Mr. Lincoln didn't love his wife?"

"That's what he told Speed before they got married."

"You know the role evil stepmothers have in fairy tales. Maybe Mr. Lincoln has chosen to be like his good stepmother since Mrs. Lincoln makes life difficult."

"I guess that makes Mary Todd the witch."

"You shouldn't be too harsh on her. Mr. Lincoln spends months out on the circuit, leaving her at home with those boys. You wouldn't be 'sweet William' to me if you spent that much time away."

Lincoln loved riding the circuit, took no notice of the bad food and corn-shuck beds, enjoyed the late nights with other lawyers and judges. Of all the riders, he was the only lawyer who visited every small town and did not come home on weekends, even after the railroad replaced his old horse. I shared a bed with him a few nights but was almost always in it and asleep before Lincoln ran out of his jokes and tales.

"Billy warms the bed out here," the other lawyers used to josh him, "but who keeps your wife warm while you're away?"

Lincoln would say, "Waal," his usual sign he was beginning a yarn or a jest. "She hires different folks to come in and take care of that."

"Are these men or womenfolk?"

"Mostly women but sometimes men."

"You let strange men sleep in your house, Lincoln?"

"Waal, they're not strange to me because it's me who pays them."

"You pay men to sleep with your wife? That's one strange form of harlotry."

"They stay awake and vigilant so she can sleep."

"What do they do all night?"

"I reckon they pray to their God she don't wake up and mistake them for me."

"Not many men in Illinois have a face like yours, Lincoln."

"That's why she prefers me at home. To scare off robbers and such."

"How long do your substitutes usually last?" would be the next question in this routine if the person were close to Lincoln, someone like Judge David Davis who also enjoyed the circuit and ribaldry.

"Mary had a cousin who lasted out a week, but one night with my wife is usually sufficient for most."

Lincoln was probably exaggerating, but the fact was that Mary hated to be alone and did require company when Lincoln was away. My wife had no such problem because I preferred to work at the office and sleep at home, maybe because my Mary and I did not quarrel, unless I took a bit too much to drink of an evening.

"I'm sure Mrs. Lincoln doesn't tolerate her husband stumbling home late."

"Lincoln doesn't drink anymore. But if Mary Todd thought his drinking would serve her ambition, she'd be giving him spirits for breakfast."

"My ambition is to see you stick by your temperance vows and be an example to the children."

Her chief desire was to see our children get more schooling than either of us had, one of the reasons I worked to establish public schools in all four sections of Springfield, tried to set up a public library, and later proposed a state university. When I was mayor, I pleased Mary and tried to help myself by forcing all the doggeries to move outside the town limits. This reduced my temptations but proved unpopular with imbibing citizens, so I served only one term. Mary Todd had no civic interest. When she came to Springfield, she was looking for a sizable man who could eventually remove her from the mud and dust of our streets. She flirted with "little Dug," Stephen A. Douglas, but he was too small. Or maybe his ambition and slipperiness exceeded Mary's. Though usually considered homely and awkward, Lincoln loomed. She saw his potential and swallowed her pride at marrying down and looking up at a man more than a foot taller than she. My Mary helped me. You might say Mary Todd whelped Lincoln, stoked his ambition, groomed him, trained him to converse politely with other women. But he never completely mastered his role for mixed company. He would walk into a party and say something like, "These ladies sure look clean" or "With this many folks, I hope they got a three-hole privy." Mary was always pushing him. She urged him to run for Congress in 1843. When there was talk in Republican circles of putting Lincoln up for vice president in 1860, Mary refused to take second place. She told her sister years before that she would marry a president, and Lincoln was going to be that man, come hell or high water. Over the years in Springfield as Lincoln rose from state legislator to representative in DC to senatorial candidate against Douglas, Mary Todd accumulated the force I wanted, but it was the wrong kind—not the pull of just ideas but the push of social prestige. As in Eden, the serpent won.

The same year I lost my partner to the presidency, I lost my Mary to tuberculosis. She had gone away to a sanitarium for some months but missed our children and returned to Springfield. The tuberculosis could not be cured, the doctors said, but I felt guilty then and feel guilty now for fathering so many children in such a short time. My sweet Mary was not strong enough to survive the motherhood she loved. Her last thoughts were for them: "Marry soon, William, our daughters need a mother." Along with grief and guilt after her passing came expense. I had to spend our meager savings to hire a woman to look after my six motherless children. At the same time, my income from the office decreased because it was Lincoln who used to bring in the big dollar clients, the railroads and other corporations we represented in the Illinois Supreme Court. I received half of those fees, but he never seemed to care. He ate poorly and dressed cheaply, both of which infuriated Mary Todd. Perhaps Lincoln did not care about what money could buy because he always had people offering him assistance—free room and board, help with his debts, campaign contributions—from the time he left his father's farm. Though he was supposed to be the realist, and I the idealist, he was more concerned with political popularity and success than with the profits other politicians filched from supporters and taxpayers. With so many children to care for after Mary's death, I had to be the practical partner, the striver and scrambler. Lincoln did get himself a dose of debt when Mary outspent his salary on foolish luxuries in the White House and then engaged in dishonest dealings to extract extra money from servants, tradesmen, and the government. I was outspending my income just to get along and had no crooked wife to bring in extra cash. When Lincoln lived in Springfield, personal economics rarely concerned him. But money worries never let me get a full night's sleep after he left the city and my sweet Mary, the woman his Mary had never been and would never be, left this earth.

CHAPTER SIX

In May of 1865 when I was doing my interviews up in New Salem, I discovered what I believe was my most significant contribution to knowledge of Lincoln's emotional makeup. I found several informants who told me about an episode in Lincoln's life that none of his biographers had written about. At the age of twenty-six, he fell in love with a blonde-haired woman by the name of Ann Rutledge, who was engaged at the time to one James McNamar. When this McNamar, whose real name was McNeil, was absent from New Salem for more than a year, Lincoln showed his interest in the nineteen-year-old beauty. For some months, Lincoln often visited Ann at her father's home, and some informants believe he was engaged to her. Then in the hot summer of 1835 Ann died of a fever. After her death, my informants told me, Lincoln "slept not, ate not, joyed not." For weeks he could do no work, walked around in a stupor when he managed to get out of bed, and his acquaintances feared for his sanity. A man named Mentor Greene said that Lincoln told him "he felt like committing suicide often." Eventually, Lincoln was taken into the care of a Mrs. Bowling Green, who helped nurse him back to health.

This tragic love, I thought, could be one important cause of Lincoln's hypos, particularly when coupled with other unhappy experiences with women such as Mary Owens and Sarah Rickard, who both refused his offer of marriage, and with the woman he married. But out of respect for Mary Todd I held back this very personal information in my first three lectures. Before making my revelation public in my fourth lecture, I wanted to give Lincoln's widow a chance to discuss his early life, psychology, and, possibly, courtships. Although I doubted she would meet with me, I took a chance and wrote Robert in the summer of 1866 to ask if his mother would allow me to talk with her for my biographical project. "I wish to do her justice fully," I said in my letter. As much as I admired Lincoln, I knew he was no easy man to have as a mate, an often abstracted and absentee husband. Mary wrote me an unexpectedly gracious reply stating that her husband's "affectionate regard for you would cause you to be cherished with the sincerest regard by my sons and myself," and, though then living in Chicago, she agreed to meet me at the Saint Nicholas Hotel in Springfield. I did not really trust this new, effusive "regard," so before our meeting I reviewed what Lincoln taught me about questioning unfriendly witnesses.

"You're going to lose your teeth," he said after watching me cross-examine a man I knew was lying. "You're like a little hound dog who has got hold of a bear and won't let go."

"I had him where I wanted, right by the ass."

"You had him, but he had the jury because you just kept chewing on his ass."

"What do you think I should have done?"

"Circle round, circle round, no barking, no show of teeth, let him git comfortable, don't dispute the little lies, wait for the whopper, and then chomp down on his neck. Or his balls if it's the end you prefer."

Since my interview of Mary Todd would possibly be the most important I conducted, I took very careful notes.

On the day of our appointment, Mrs. Lincoln was sitting in the lobby of the Saint Nicholas dressed all in black and wearing a hat with a veil that covered her face. I did not recognize her, and she had to call to me across the lobby. "Mr. Herndon, Mr. Herndon," no longer Lincoln's Billy. From what I could see behind her veil, she appeared much diminished in health, her usually round face more angular, like Lincoln's. Her hand was cold and slightly trembling, and her voice was almost a whisper after she called to me.

"You are looking well," she said, and I told her, "I have not really been well since our Mr. Lincoln passed."

"None of us who loved him shall ever be well again."

I agreed, summarized my first two lectures, and described my planned biography, which I hoped would keep alive something of the true Lincoln that we both revered. I told her about some of my researches into his life before Springfield and asked if she would tell me what she knew.

"As you may know," she said, "Mr. Lincoln said very little about his early life. For the longest time, I didn't know he had been a river pilot. I fear I cannot help you with those years."

"Did he ever talk with you about his trips to New Orleans?"

"Not that I recall."

"And you know nothing about his time in New Salem?"

"Only that he clerked in a store and began his study of the law there, which I'm sure you already know."

I doubted Mary's ignorance but did not press her as I might have a witness. I would change tacks and return to my real interest.

"Could I ask you, then, a few questions about your life with Mr. Lincoln?"

"Mr. Lincoln was the greatest president the United States has ever had, Mr. Herndon. My life is of no importance. I feel it would not be proper to be discussed in the biography of a president."

I wondered about her sincerity. Since she never dodged public attention, I suspected she was reluctant to be represented by someone who already knew much about her life with her husband. But I still wanted to give her the opportunity to offer her view.

"But, you see," I said, "my biography will be somewhat different from the usual recitation of facts about appointments and elections and battles. It will include those facts but will also analyze the president's psychology, which you could discuss better than anyone."

Willy-nilly Billy, as Lincoln used to say about my excess of words. With the mention of "psychology," the woman who would spend time in an asylum drew back in her chair and shook her head. She maintained her gracious manner, but I realized I had misspoken. I would not be able to ask Mary about Lincoln's hypos. I tried to recover by asking for just a brief portrait of her life before she met Mr. Lincoln.

"My life began when I met my future husband," she said. That did not correspond to what I knew about Mary Todd fielding suitors in Springfield, but I did not argue with her. I just said, "I understand how you feel. I feel the same way, but I also have a birth date I celebrate every year."

"Well, Mr. Herndon, if you must. I was born on the thirteenth of December, 1823." She went on to give some basic information about her family in Kentucky, her education, and her life with her sister in Springfield. Both sisters had left their home because, she said, they were not "in full sympathy with our father or our stepmother." Mary warmed to talking about herself, so I took another chance.

"Would you say a few words about Mr. Lincoln's courtship when you were living with your sister?"

"That, sir," she said in the cutting tone of old, "is a private matter that no man should ask a woman about."

At that time, of course, I knew why she refused to discuss the embarrassing events leading up to her marriage—the broken engagement, the secret second courtship, the hurry-up wedding, the gingerbread instead of a proper wedding cake, the honeymoon at the Globe Hotel in town. Later, checking facts, I discovered that she had put forward her birth by five years. I had not even had to "chomp down" on her. She lied gratuitously, out of vanity.

During the rest of our hour together, she insisted on talking about Lincoln in the White House. This was a Lincoln I only partly recognized, a generous and kind-hearted man, yes, but not one she claimed "enjoyed our domestic felicity" or one "whose manners became quite polished." Her voice regained some of its Mrs. President authority as she discussed improvements in Lincoln for which she seemed to expect credit. I became impatient with her and decided to see just how much I could trust Mary Todd by asking about Mr. Lincoln's faith. Mary said he was "always a religious man" but then, much to my surprise, admitted he was "not a technical Christian." I believe she regretted telling that latter truth as much as I regretted saying "psychology" earlier because immediately after confessing what I already knew, Mrs. Lincoln sighed, slumped in her chair, and disappeared into the role of the Martyr's Widow. She said, "Mr. Herndon, talking about my husband is still very painful to me. Can we stop now and perhaps speak another day?"

We never spoke again. I had not expected that Ann Rutledge could enter our conversation, but after Mary Todd's friendly letter I allowed myself to hope for more cooperation, even if only general. I did not require that cooperation. In October of 1866, I went back to New Salem and interviewed the man to whom Ann Rutledge had been engaged and visited her grave. From my informants, I had enough facts to make the Ann Rutledge story the centerpiece of the lecture I gave in November of 1866. My revelation of Lincoln's long-lost love might have been accepted, perhaps even welcomed as a romantic episode, but my conclusions set off the mines. After describing the death of Miss Rutledge, I used my knowledge of how Lincoln signed his letters—without using the words "affectionately" or "love"—to imply what I knew as a fact: that he could never truly love another woman. I knew that he did not love Mary Todd and that his honor drove him into a near-suicidal hypo in 1841 before he finally married her, but I did not put these facts into the lecture. "One mine at a time," Anna suggested. My intents were to show one historic cause of Lincoln's domestic unhappiness and to suggest at least one cause of his hypos, though I knew more that I wished to reserve for my biography. As I wrote to several persons at the time, I wanted a friend of Lincoln to reveal his unhappy past, to explain it in the best of lights, because I knew that soon Lincoln's enemies would be attempting for partisan gain to undermine the inaccurate idealization got up by the eulogists. And as I wrote to Hart, my young bibliographer, I wanted to be fair to Mary Todd, to suggest why Lincoln and she were a bad match: "She hates me," I wrote Hart, "yet I can and will do her justice . . . Poor woman! The world has no charity for her, and yet justice must be done her." She had lived with a husband that his honor or her ambition netted her.

Not even my cautious Anna predicted the poison that was poured in her husband's ears after the Ann Rutledge lecture. People who praised my first two lectures turned on me. Those who knew Lincoln did not question my facts but were incensed by the impropriety of my revelation. Friends snubbed me on the street or insulted my honor. A good friend of Anna told her, "Shame on you and your husband," as if Anna and I were coauthors of the lecture. Several former clients asked how I could betray my dead partner. Francis Carpenter, the man who used material from my first lectures in his book, wrote that this lecture was an "invasion of the sacred chamber." Newspapers all over the United States carried reports of the lecture, and most were brutal in their attacks on me, always on the ground of impropriety, making the private public. I was hurt and angry. And I did not understand. Lincoln was a public man. He often joked in public about a man's or a woman's privates. I included in my lecture nothing like this, nothing vulgar. I felt I was following Lincoln's example, his love of truth and dislike of sham politeness. I also believed that the "proper privacy" being shouted against me offered men a cover for possibly immoral actions they wanted to keep secret. Women also hid behind "propriety," as if their bodies or physical desires or intimate relations did not exist. I felt I had handled Lincoln's personal history with some delicacy. I had even crossed out of my lecture draft a more explicit assertion about his unhappiness. But just as it was too soon to fully reveal Lincoln's religious skepticism, it was too early to suggest that the Great Emancipator had been less than free from his past love and less than joyful in his marriage.

Remarks meant primarily for residents of Springfield spread out across the nation and even abroad. James Smith, the former minister of the First Presbyterian Church, where Mary used to attend services, read an account of my lecture in Dundee, Scotland. News of my "sin" had leaped across the ocean! Although Smith knew nothing of Lincoln, he published a letter in that city's newspaper that attacked me on both religious and domestic issues. Reverend Smith employed his knowledge of the Biblical Abraham to contrast Lincoln and me. Old Abraham had broken graven idols; I had attempted to smash a sacred idol of America. Smith also likened me to John Wilkes Booth. His letter leaped back across the Atlantic to be republished in the *Chicago Tribune*, where Mary Todd could read it.

In December, Mary dispatched Robert to Springfield to silence me. I had always felt that Robert was a Todd, an odd, lonely mama's boy in need of more attention than he received from Lincoln, with whom the boy could be standoffish, formal like a young prince. When Robert was at Harvard, I wrote him friendly letters of advice that he never acknowledged. I knew that the Lincolns had opposed his enlisting in the war, and I respected Robert for insisting, though his father managed to find a safe perch for him with General Grant.

Robert was about my height, not imposing like his father, though when he entered my office his back was stiff and he was dressed in a better suit than Lincoln ever owned before he became president. The army must have taught him his new firm handshake. Not much had changed in the office, which I thought might please Robert, but when I pointed to his father's couch Robert refused to sit.

"My business here will be brief, Mr. Herndon," he said.

"Business, Robert? Did you have a suit you came all the way from Chicago to discuss with an old country lawyer?"

"Not a suit but a request that I trust you will grant without a suit."

Robert's speech was as stiff and formal as his bearing and clothes.

"Waal, as your father the peacemaker used to say to clients, 'Let's see if your facts fly?'"

"My facts, Mr. Herndon? I am here about your 'facts' and your errors of judgment."

I sat behind my desk with my hands on my chair arms, appearing relaxed and confident as Lincoln taught me by example. Standing, Robert had no place to rest his arms, and he began hitting his left palm with his right fist. I believed Robert, like my brother in his office, wanted to fight me, but I gave him no one to fight. I stayed silent, one of my partner's tricks, and forced Robert to explain himself.

"My mother and I believe you are reporting gossip, not facts, from my father's New Salem years. The conclusions you draw from this gossip and the aspersions you cast upon my parents' marital relation are offensive and hurtful to my widowed mother and to me. We request that you cease and desist."

I tried to calm Robert with one of Lincoln's evasive devices. "Your father would be proud of you and your Harvard education," I told him. "I'm pretty sure neither one of us knew the word 'aspersions' until we were in our thirties."

"I did not come all this way to be joked with. I insist that you respond to our request."

"If you like, Robert, I can show you my interview notes from New Salem, including my talk with Miss Rutledge's former fiancé, Mr. McNamar, who still lives up there. As for my conclusions, I reckon I spent more waking hours with your father than you did, but surely you observed strife at home. Perhaps you did not see your mother chase your father in the yard with a butcher knife or hit him with a piece of firewood when he ignored her. But facts I'm sure you will recall are your visits to this office with your father early in those mornings when he was driven out of your home by your mother. I distinctly remember you and him eating breakfasts of crackers and cheese on that long couch your father purchased so he could spend nights in the office when your mother was on the warpath."

My reference to Robert's own experience deflated a bit his puffed-out chest.

"Think of propriety, Mr. Herndon."

"Your father didn't think much of it. He once told me, 'I think I could be a proper gentleman if I could just hide that damned monkey's tail I inherited.'"

"Then think of a widow in deep distress. I ask you, as a man who loved my father, not to cause the woman he loved any further suffering. I appeal to your honor, Mr. Herndon."

"Your father was honorable with your mother, and yet she made him suffer for more than two decades."

"Even if that were so, my father has been buried for less than two years. It is too soon to be delving into these very private matters."

"Already biographies full of errors about your father have been published, Robert, which may prove that you are right. I had hoped to forestall further errors, but I will give 'due consideration,' as we lawyers say, to your request as I work on my book."

"My mother spoke with me about your interview with her. From the questions you asked, she believes you are writing this book for profit, since you no longer have my father to depend on in this office."

"And what about you, Robert, what do you believe?"

Robert looked around the office, still as shabby and cluttered as when his father worked here. I couldn't bear to move anything.

"My father cared little for money, and it appears that you don't either. Perhaps you hope to have some fame in the world," he said. "Your sign outside still reads 'Lincoln and Herndon.' Your book would spread the sign's suggested equality far and wide."

"My name is beneath your father's, and I was always the junior partner. But you and your mother have learned your father's belief about motivation well. He used to lie over on that sofa and argue with me about selfishness. He maintained that every human action was ultimately selfish. It was an odd belief for someone with the great stores of charity your father possessed—and displayed toward your mother. I think he got this idea from Locke, and no matter how much Hume I applied I could not get him to admit the possibility of altruism. We had many a go-round about altruism. He wanted me to give it up, but I still believe in it."

Here I stopped to see if I needed any more history before I closed with a notion I knew Robert would not accept. Maybe he read no Locke or Hume up in Cambridge. He looked impatient. So I went on ahead with my conclusion: "My biography is for your father and, indirectly, for you and your mother because it will be the truthful basis of all future biographies. You will, I fear, just have to trust me as your father did."

"He trusted you as his law partner, Mr. Herndon."

"He trusted me as his friend, Robert. That was enough for your father."

"But as his partner and his friend, you were often drunk. My mother has told me this and believes you are therefore not qualified to be the president's biographer."

"Grant was often drunk and won the war for your father. I was entirely sober here in this office when your father told me about events in his life that you and your mother know nothing about."

"If what you say is true, Mr. Herndon, I hope we never learn about these events from you. My mother and I know that you differed radically with my father on the issue of slavery, and we fear that you will not be fair to the man who emancipated the slaves."

Robert came all the way from Chicago to have the last word, and I gave it to him, even though his last sentence angered me more than anything else he said. I could have told him many a story about his father, but I didn't. Poor Robert, I thought, as his boots clattered down the stairs. Deputized by a mother ruled by the selfishness that Lincoln maintained ruled everyone, the Martyr's Son might eventually get free of her but never of the role she had assigned him as protector of a myth. "*Veritas*" was the motto of Robert's Harvard, but it was a motto that his circumstances made impossible to observe. But perhaps Lincoln was right about universal and inescapable selfishness. Writing my notes on this conversation, I was pleased with myself that I did not say to the honor-appealing Robert that it was honor, and only honor, not love, that gave him Abraham Lincoln as a father. Robert would have to live with what he knew about his mother. I allowed him ignorance of his father's suicidal depression when faced with the prospect of marrying Mary Todd. And more than two decades later, I did not include these detailed memoirs of gaunt Mary Todd and puffy Robert Lincoln in my biography.

I also did not include a story about the youthful Lincoln I could have told his son. When Lincoln came to our office on his last day in Springfield, he told me he would be back, and then he asked me, "How many times have you been drunk, Billy?"

I believe he was worried about the office of Lincoln and Herndon, and he was right to be because I answered, "You probably know the answer better than I do, Mr. Lincoln. There are times I don't remember much."

Lincoln nodded and then the president-elect took the time to tell his Billy a story.

Lincoln said his father used to drink corn in the winter to, Thomas Lincoln said, "stay warm inside," which meant he did not always keep the stove supplied with chunk wood.

"Before I split rails, Billy, I split frozen blocks out in the snow. Neither my mother or stepmother drank, and that angered my father, who swore at them for ruining his pleasure with their sour faces." According to Lincoln, most men in Kentucky and Indiana, except for some of the Baptists, drank, and some "grocery" stores, one of his included, sold mostly liquor and tobacco. Men would get drunk for a few days, but in these villages where life was hard nobody was allowed to get very far out of plumb. When Gentry and Lincoln left on their flatboat, they had hogs and hominy to sell, corn liquor to drink during those long dark evenings on the Mississippi. The night they were attacked by slaves, Lincoln said, they had more than a few draws off the jug.

When they reached New Orleans, they were amazed at the number of taverns and the number of drunken men walking the streets, singing songs in languages the Kaintucks did not understand, falling down on the wooden sidewalks or in the gutters, vomiting or urinating on themselves.

Gentry says to Raymond, "These must be sailors up from downriver."

"Some," Raymond says. "But look at their clothes. Many are flatboaters happy to be escaped from wives and preachers. Liquor is cheap down here. Some of it comes from good old Kaintucky corn, some is brought up from the Carib. Have you boys ever had rum?"

"Shoot, Raymond," Lincoln says, "I ain't even had a woman yet."

"Me neither," Gentry says, "if a ewe don't count."

"Rum will cost you boys less, and you won't catch the syph."

"So," Lincoln said, "the three of us got to a tavern and went to pouring that rum down our gullets. It tasted a whole lot better than corn, and soon Gentry and I were skunked. Raymond was used to the rum and was all right. He was trying to herd us out the door when I run up against a little bald feller coming in. Waal, he took offense and took a swing at me. But this boy didn't have no club like that slave. So I got hold of him to wrassle him down to the floor where I could press the piss and vinegar out of him."

Here Lincoln paused and then asked, "Do you know the 'Indian Hug' hold?"

"I never wrassled with your Clary's Grove boys up in New Salem."

"You wrap your arms around the other feller and dig your chin into his collarbone. Tall as I am that hold never failed me, but that rum made me dumb and slow, and the little feller slipped right out of that hug and quick legged me, putting me on my back as easy as you'd tip over a milking stool. My head thumped the wood, and Gentry and Raymond said the feller bounced it a few more times before they could pry him off me."

"I thought indomitable Abe had never been taken down."

"Waal, I don't count it, Billy. I warn't myself. It was rum not that bald boy put me on my back."

Then Lincoln dropped his Kaintuck story voice and became earnest. "I'm no temperance lecturer, Billy. You know what too much drink can cost a man. It cost me when I paid for those windows you broke in Green's tavern. But the big cost is not in your pocket. It's in your head. If Gentry and Raymond weren't along, that feller could have bounced my head until the brains spilled out. That's what drinking does. Bounces your brains so you're not wrassling with another feller but wrassling against yourself. You're two people inside, so you lose yourself. That one bouncing was enough for me. If I were going to rise in the world like Raymond, I'd need all my brains. So the next day, when my brains felt somewhere near normal I swore at spirits and then swore off them."

Lincoln did not like to lecture unless politics were involved, so he swung back into his Kaintuck voice:

"Waal, Billy, with me up there in the White House you're going to need all the brains you got here by yourself. And now that you abolitionists got us near into a war, I'll be expecting you and your brains to tell me how to git out of it without getting shot myself."

That last sentence I remember as exactly as his promise to return to Lincoln and Herndon. He was joshing about me and "my" abolitionists causing the war, and yet somewhere in that line of a million causes for his assassination I had some responsibility for Lincoln being shot in the brain. Sober during the war years, I admit I often found comfort in spirits after Lincoln's death. While my drinking did at times delay the writing of my biography, I believe alcohol never influenced my perceptions and memories of my friend and partner. My drinking was another "impropriety" to be used against me when people, like the Lincolns, feared what I could or did reveal about the president.

CHAPTER SEVEN

More disturbing to me than Robert's statement about my drinking was his accusation based on slavery. It was indeed the matter over which Lincoln and I differed most, causing some lengthy political disagreements but never a serious rift in our friendship. Because slavery was the most important issue of our age, I want to clarify when and how Lincoln and I disagreed. Lincoln's public positions on abolition I reported in the biography. Here are facts and conversations that were left out of *Herndon's Lincoln*.

When I first became Lincoln's partner, I used to bring William Lloyd Garrison's abolitionist newspaper the *Liberator* to the office and read its eloquent passages aloud to Lincoln because I knew it was not a paper he would ever choose to read to me. For as long as I knew Lincoln, he was emotionally opposed to slavery, but he could be inconsistent in his actions. For some years, he claimed abolitionists helped perpetuate the slavery they opposed, and he was against Negro suffrage in New York and in Illinois. He represented the slave owner Robert Matson in a suit to recover slaves, and Lincoln campaigned for another slave owner, Zachary Taylor, when he ran for president. Lincoln once said, "God will settle slavery, and it is our duty to wait"—an odd statement because he did not believe in a providential deity who sorted out human affairs. Lincoln publicly supported the damnable Fugitive Slave Act, though he opposed it in private. He was slow to speak out for strong government policies that would prevent slavery from spreading to western states and territories—and slower yet to favor the end of slavery in the Union. Right up to the Emancipation Proclamation, he accepted the constitutional right of slaveholders to hold slaves. His Kentucky wife sympathized with the slavocrats. Mary Todd once said that if she lost her husband, she wanted to live in a slave state. "That's why," my Mary used to tell me, "you must keep Mr. Lincoln's feet to the fire." But Lincoln was a cautious man whose feet were far from his heart and difficult to heat.

At times during our partnership I was enthusiastic about temperance and women's rights, neither of which much interested Lincoln, but about slavery I was unapologetically passionate. My college professors introduced me to abolitionist writings by Charles Sumner, Henry Ward Beecher, Wendell Phillips, Theodore Parker. These were the men who warmed my heart. Later I joined the Whig Party, as did Lincoln, because of its anti-slavery positions. It was the repeal of the Missouri Compromise in 1854 and the threat of Kansas becoming a slave state that fired my soul. Lincoln and I broke with the old Whigs, and in 1856 he put me on the founding committee of the new Illinois Republican Party with its more enlightened policy toward slavery. Then came the Supreme Court's infamous Dred Scott decision in 1857 that ruled Congress could not limit the expansion of slavery into new states and that Negroes were not citizens and therefore could not sue in United States courts. Lincoln opposed the first provision but lawyered around the second with a peculiar construction of the Declaration's "all men are created equal." Negroes were equal in their right to profit from their labor, he said, but he denied the full equality of Negroes. "Free the slaves and make them politically and socially our equals?" he asked in a debate with Stephen A. Douglas. "My own feelings will not admit of this," Lincoln said. In 1857 Lincoln's solution to the problem of slavery was colonization, sending Negroes back to Africa. I believe he knew this would never work, but proposing putting Negroes in ships allowed him to avoid more realistic but difficult "solutions."

After Dred Scott, my feelings were abraded and people in Springfield knew it. Some accused me of harboring runaway slaves in our office while they waited to move along the freedom railway to Canada. I wish I had, but Lincoln would never have approved. I wrote to Theodore Parker that "if the South will tap the dinner gong and call the wild, bony, quick, brave peoples to a feast of civil war, and make this land quiver and ring from center to circumference, then I can but say the quicker the better." But Lincoln resisted what Seward called the "irrepressible conflict" until Fort Sumter. I favored war to end slavery and preserve the Union even if war meant pitting brother against brother as happened that year in Springfield where we had our own Dred Scott case. A fugitive slave was arrested north of the capital and brought before the United States commissioner in Springfield, who would rule whether or not he should be returned to his owner in Kentucky. I quickly volunteered to represent the poor man without charge. Much to my chagrin, my brother, Elliott, then agreed to represent the fugitive's owner. Like my father, Elliott was a Democrat, and we often conflicted over state and national politics, but this was a personal provocation. I walked the two blocks to Elliott's office to ask him why.

"Counselor," he addressed me in a mocking tone, "you must know that any plaintiff has the right to legal representation."

"An attorney has the right to refuse representation, Elliott. Why would you try to send a man back into a life of bondage and misery?"

"According to the statutes of Illinois, an owner has the right to sue for defense of his property."

"A man is not a horse and wagon or four acres over by the Sangamon."

"There is some doubt that a nigger is a man."

"If a man is defined as a creature walking on two legs, you with your crutches are also not a man, Elliott."

Elliott's legs had been crooked since birth. He picked up the crutches that leaned against his desk and shook them at me. "You have come to this, have you, insulting my dignity as a man? Is this the kind of argument your partner taught you? Can you not keep to the law?"

"I know the damned law, Elliott. You have chosen this to spite me, your own brother. You don't care about the fugitive or the law, only the chance to provoke me and other Republicans. It's a shameful thing you do. And unmanly."

"Get out, Will, go back to your nigger-loving amalgamationist partner."

Democratic editors and politicians like Douglas routinely called Republicans "nigger-lovers" and proponents of miscegenation, but Elliott's insult was personal, directed at a man he saw every week at the courthouse. Had Elliott not needed his crutches to walk, I believe we would have come to blows there in his office.

When we appeared before the commissioner, Elliott attempted to deny the fugitive his right to my representation. That failed, but the case was decided on narrow grounds in favor of the plaintiff and Elliott. The fugitive, like Dred Scott, was returned to slavery. Lincoln said after the decision, "You fought the good fight, Billy, but the laws were agin you."

"That's the reason," I told him, "the laws must be changed in North and South."

"The Constitution is not an ordinance people can change on a whim from season to season."

"The Constitution was partly written by slaveholders. It's not like the Bible. It can be rewritten. Get it more in line with the Declaration."

"Not all races are equal in their capabilities."

"How will we know if that's true if every Dred Scott is returned to a state where he will see no profit from his labors or develop his capabilities?"

"It's a noble position, your equality, but we will not see it tested in our lifetimes, Billy, because no politician can be elected on a platform with equality as a plank."

"Then maybe we need another 1776 now or in 1876 when we'll both be alive to see it. We can have a Declaration of Equality."

"You and your abolitionist friends can declare it just like folks declare the moon is made of blue cheese, but it will never happen."

For Lincoln inequality was not just one of the planks he pretended to stand on to get votes. Inequality of the races was no blue cheese but bedrock belief for him, and none of my science or Garrison's eloquence could persuade him otherwise. Like the friendship of Crusoe and Friday, equality was a fiction to Lincoln.

"What about your New Orleans?" I asked Lincoln. "There are a lot of free blacks down there who aren't just servants like your friend Raymond's. I've read Negroes are storekeepers and tradesmen and even doctors."

This was the only time I ever asked Lincoln a direct question about New Orleans. He looked displeased, as if I were trespassing on his stories.

"I don't know, Billy. Maybe there are Negro root doctors, but I didn't run into any black lawyers like you and me. Almost all the Negroes I saw were sweating, laboring on the docks or in the streets. I suppose they were equal to white laborers, but you don't find many of them in New Orleans. I never saw any white folks in the chain gangs either."

"If they were chained, they were slaves. Some of them might have been like Dred Scott, free for a time but returned to bondage. Didn't such sights make you want to leave right away?"

"I'd never been to a city, and I was young. I was having a merry time down there. Gentry wanted to get back home. I didn't, not then. But after my second trip with that fool Offutt, I started having a dream about leaving. I still have it some nights. I'm on a flatboat, ready to go home. I got the sail on the boat rigged up, and I'm hauling away at my oar, but I can't beat that current. But it can't beat me. It's like that boat is on dry land. I'm stuck still in the middle of the Mississip."

"Where are Offutt and Johnston? They're not helping?"

"Seems like I'm all alone, but I can hear squealing that don't sound like hogs. And I can hear Negro voices from the shore laughing and calling out in the night."

"What are they saying?"

"I can't make them out. It's all confusion, like the night Gentry and I was attacked, and I ain't moving ahead."

"Maybe you didn't really want to leave."

"That ain't it because I'm sweating on that oar and cursing that damn current. I want to git back upriver but can't."

"I wouldn't worry it," I told him, "you're on dry land in Springfield now."

"During the day, Billy, but not always at night."

Two years after the Dred Scott decision, John Brown and his band of abolitionists raided Harpers Ferry. I felt Brown would, as I wrote to Parker, "live amidst the world's gods and heroes through all the ages." Lincoln had lost his Senate bid to Douglas the year before but still held high political ambitions, so he publicly repudiated Brown, and we had the only heated argument in our long, congenial partnership and friendship. Most of our work was defense, but Lincoln spoke as if he were prosecuting a case before a judge, not telling a story in the office or on the circuit. Brown's attack on the armory was, Lincoln said, a "violation of state and federal statutes." I countered with Seward's famous defense of "higher laws" than statutes.

"You and I and Seward agree," Lincoln said, "that slavery is a moral evil, but old man Brown set back moral progress with his means."

"Were they not the means colonists used against the Redcoats?"

"Ah, your revolution again. The United States government is not a colonial ruler."

"I'll wager two dollars to two bits that slaves don't see the difference between white Englishmen and white Americans."

"But the violent means of Brown failed, not just to hold the armory but to hive white sympathizers to his cause. In was an insurrection not a revolution."

"Socrates failed. Jesus failed. We can't dismiss Brown now because he failed. Like those sacrificed heroes, his courage and ideals will inspire people in the future."

"Brown couldn't even inspire more than a few Negroes to join his band."

"Free blacks fought with Brown and gave their lives for the cause."

"Yes, but not slaves. They were not ready."

"They were not free, Mr. Lincoln."

"I wouldn't think you'd want to support a Christian zealot, Billy."

"I don't care if a man is reading the Bible or the Declaration of Independence to his followers, as long as he strikes the necessary blow."

"He struck no blow against slaveholders. Only the government, and innocent citizens were killed."

"If government troops had not surrounded him, he and his men would have used the guns in that armory to fire on the man-stealers on their plantations."

"You've not been to war. Brown was trying to start one."

"I was too young to chase poor old Black Hawk around the bushes as you did, but I would have fought had that conflict been just. If I were a single man, I would have saddled a horse with Brown."

Lincoln slowly shook his head, as if disappointed in the law-breaking young law student he had taken on as his partner.

"Old man Brown was insane, Billy."

I had never heard Lincoln descend to this kind of *ad hominem*, maybe on the stump before a foot-stomping crowd but never in our serious conversations. From what I know now from my informants, his remark was also hypocritical because during two periods of Lincoln's life he, too, had been considered "insane," if only temporarily so.

"That is not worthy of you, Mr. Lincoln. You reduce a courageous and heroic man to an illness. He was a victim in bloody Kansas. He has put spine and steel into his conscience. He has given to his grand cause the lives of two sons. His family will be outcasts, and he will be hanged like a common criminal. Old man Brown of Kansas has done something neither of us young men of Illinois has done. Brown acted on his beliefs without considering the effects on voters."

"Billy," he said, "you are too rampant and spontaneous."

Lincoln had teased me before about my enthusiasms, my Injin Bill provocations and my gobble gobble, but this time he was not joking. I was taken aback and silent. This time Lincoln's use of "Billy" felt condescending and unfair. To justify his *ad hominem* against me, he embarked on a long disquisition about political effects: how I had not considered that southern Democrats would trump up charges that Brown was a Republican agent, that Republicans would be tarred with the slave insurrection brush, that Brown could hurt Republican chances in the upcoming presidential election. Lincoln had been mentioned by other Republicans and editors as a possible presidential candidate in 1860. With Brown, as with other issues concerning slavery, Lincoln betrayed his just sentiments to his lawyerly logic and the political ambition I saw in the East. About slavery, he wrote to his friend Speed that he, a Southerner, should appreciate how Northerners "crucify their feelings in order to maintain their loyalty to the Constitution and the Union." I saw no crucifixion in Lincoln's comments on John Brown. I understood Lincoln's need to keep private feelings and public pronouncements separate, but this time his personal belief greatly disappointed me. After the war began and Union soldiers were singing "John Brown's Body," I sent a brief note to Lincoln in the White House: "John Brown's body lies amouldering in the grave, but his spirit marches on."

Despite our disagreement about Brown, Lincoln was the nation's only hope against slavery in 1860. His voice was not commanding, but his speeches, even ones he had not prepared, were powerful in their knowledge and morality. What he could do telling stories on the circuit and influencing juries in the courtroom he could also do on the stump. He had the effect of a deep well whose bottom you could not see. People leaned toward him as if peering over the edge. I worked hard for him but had no official position with the campaign. Herndon had through his associations with abolitionists and his admiration for John Brown become untrustworthy as a spokesman. Lincoln's Billy was too spontaneous. I was allowed to stump in Illinois backwater towns but not to speak for the candidate as I had always done before.

When Lincoln was in Springfield, he would come over to our office from his campaign headquarters to discuss cases that were still pending or to collect his half of our fees. He might tell a story or two, but he was no longer a country lawyer. He was always pressed for time and eventually called back by some underling. It was a very contradictory period for me. My partner might become president of the United States, but I seemed to be losing my best friend. Race and his race for the highest office in the land had pried open a space between us. We had often butted heads over the best way to resolve the "Negro Problem," and I believe Lincoln valued my summations of abolitionist arguments. But his political ambition was not something I could argue with. I wanted him to be president but not to leave Lincoln and Herndon. In the end, my force could not counteract Mary Todd's. When he won, Marymax and I joined the jubilation but with the foreknowledge of loss. That is the reason I was so pleased with Lincoln's promise to come back from Washington and practice law with me.

I saw Lincoln one more time after he left for Washington. When he was in the White House, we frequently corresponded about firm business but he rarely wrote about politics. I took the hint but once or twice wrote long letters urging him to emancipate the slaves. To these letters I received no reply. Perhaps they were intercepted by his secretaries, Nicolay and Hay, who called Lincoln the "tycoon" and treated him like one, not like a man who had been elected to a public office. When I visited him in January of 1862, slavery was still legal in the District, and Lincoln was busy studying military strategies and still receiving persons who wanted to secure some government position. Rumor was that Mary was on a spending spree decorating the White House up to her Lexington standards of elegance. Their new home did not impress me much. Every room was cold, and I was disgusted by the patronage seekers lining the hallways. If being misled by generals and hounded by beggars were political success, I was glad to have failed in politics.

I do believe Lincoln enjoyed having an old familiar to whom he could retell stories. He even introduced me to cabinet members as his "law partner and old friend," but he cut me short when I tried to bring up emancipation as a just principle: "This damned war will be over one day, Billy, and we will have to live again with citizens of the South. Even if we compensated the secessionists for their losses, we would never again be a Union." When I visited the White House, William Herndon was still impractical Billy, Mary Maxcy was dead, and I was no "William Wilson." Lincoln's cabinet now did his research and gave him his advice. I knew how he had chosen them, bringing enemies close, and I wondered if he could trust any one of them. His only partner was the rampant and spontaneous Mary Todd, whom Lincoln referred to as "Mrs. President." Much to his eventual regret, Lincoln trusted her with money, and she became a thief.

I knew I had failed as a city man when I ran short of cash and had to join the petitioners—to borrow twenty-five dollars from the president of the United States. He joked, "We'll jes charge it to the national debt," but I was still embarrassed. I believe he was embarrassed that Mrs. President did not offer to entertain me in the Lincolns' private quarters. I saw her leaving Lincoln's office one morning, and she nodded but did not speak. She I would see once more under very different circumstances—when it was in the serpent's interest to be polite to Billy. After my week in the District, Lincoln was fond and hearty bidding me farewell. He squeezed my hand like an ax handle and said, "Billy, you hold the fort out there on the frontier, and I'll skin the rebels from here." But like Lincoln on many occasions, I had a presentiment: I would not see him again. Even when talking of old times and places, he seemed somewhere else, neither there nor here. He often forgot his "Kaintuck" accent when telling stories, and yet he did not seem comfortable in his role as chief executive. His jokes and riddles were more pessimistic. He asked me, "What's the difference between a man to be hanged and a president?" The answer was, "They tell the hanged man before it happens." Already his face was more lined and his expression more melancholy, as if he were ill or battling a persistent hypo. Lincoln slumping behind his desk in the White House and bemoaning the war's toll was far removed from Lincoln sprawling on our office sofa and talking excitedly about his ambition inspiring trip to New Orleans. I felt sorry for my friend the president of the United States.

CHAPTER EIGHT

The vicious attacks on my propriety and respectability after the Ann Rutledge lecture demonstrated to me, if not to Anna, that I was on the right trail with my revelations about Lincoln's "subjective" life. The two Lincolns' opposition also showed the value of my unconventional undertaking. I was "walking with clean boots," as Lincoln used to say when his mood was good. And besides, not everyone attacked "that ass Herndon," as Robert later called me, for my Ann Rutledge lecture. The famous newspaper reporter and columnist George Alfred Townsend interviewed me in Springfield. Anna and I were not very pleased with his description of me, though I admit I liked his last line:

"A saffron-faced, blue-black haired man bearded bushily at the throat, disposed to shut one eye for accuracy in conversation, his teeth discolored by tobacco, and over his angular features, which suggested Mr. Lincoln's in ampleness and shape, the same half-tender melancholy."

"Gath," Townsend's pen name, admitted his notions of Lincoln's character were "staggered" by my informants' interviews but wrote up a very complimentary report of our conversation that appeared on the front page of the *New York Tribune*. Because of his article's popularity, it was reprinted in the weekly *Independent* and later appeared as a pamphlet entitled "The Real Life of Abraham Lincoln." Although Gath embellished some of the facts I told him, I was honored by a fellow writer's recognition of my project: a "Real Life" of its subject.

Even more supportive than Gath was Caroline Dall. Mrs. Dall and I began corresponding in 1860 about women's rights, for which she was a more faithful crusader than I, and about abolition, for which, I believe, we were equally passionate. In 1866 she was on a lecture tour of the Midwest, and I invited her to Springfield to give a lecture, the more iconoclastic the better. Mrs. Dall was a guest in our home, and we had many hours of inspirational conversation about the prairie and Lincoln as a son of the West. I liked Mrs. Dall a great deal. Like me, she was an enthusiast. She also looked like my notion of a daughter of the East. Her dress was Puritan severe, and she pulled her dark hair back into a very proper bun. She seemed to have never stepped out of her library into the sun. She pronounced vowels as Garrison did. Anna asked if all women from the East were as plain in appearance as Mrs. Dall, but I believe my wife just did not like to have another writer in the house. I told Mrs. Dall about my Ann Rutledge lecture and my ambitions for my biography.

"Miss Rutledge will make a romantic story for your book," Mrs. Dall said, "but not one that advances the cause of women. She's like all those maidens in novels who are too pure for this world. It's unfortunate Mrs. Lincoln is not a more sympathetic figure."

"Or a more pure figure."

"From what I have read, she was a strong-willed woman despite her tragedies. Perhaps with her husband gone, she will contribute to the suffrage movement. Imagine her standing in a hall full of women and saying, 'I am not free to vote though my husband freed the slaves.'"

"That wouldn't be a lie, at least."

"Mrs. Lincoln lies?"

"Let's say she is unreliable. But I can imagine Mary Todd saying what you want if the ladies group paid her a handsome fee. You should not expect much from her, but I want to be fair to her in my book. Lincoln was a great president but only a so-so husband."

"Was he unfaithful?"

"No, though he surely had his chances on the circuit. He used to say, 'It's a good thing I'm not a woman because I can't say no.'"

"But you believe he did say no to other women?"

"Yes, but would never say no to a chance to be away from home—lawyering on the circuit, giving speeches for others, debating and politicking."

"You must be fair to both—the truth about both—for the book to help bring about the equality of women and men."

After Mrs. Dall left Springfield, I wrote her that "No one in the world but you so well knows my trials, plans, and schemes"—partly because of an incident that was embarrassing at the time but now appears fortunate. One day when I was out of the house, Mrs. Dall was looking through interviews with my informants when she found two black notebooks where I had been recording doubtful rumors about Lincoln, some of his more vulgar jokes, and stories about his trips to New Orleans that I wanted to remember in detail because the revelations were so unusual for the shut-mouthed Lincoln. Anna discovered Mrs. Dall reading these notebooks and told her she must stop and give them over. Perhaps out of misplaced politeness or fear of what I might say to Mrs. Dall, Anna did not tell me of the incident until after Mrs. Dall left for her next lecture in Wisconsin. Although I was upset with Anna at the time, I now see the benefit of her silence. I immediately wrote Mrs. Dall, explained the notebooks, and swore her to secrecy about them, which she promised in her apologetic response. The benefit is this: I now have correspondence confirming the existence of the black notebooks should anyone reading this book doubt the truth of my recollections drawn from the notebooks.

Although Mrs. Dall was, she said, "singed" by some of my informants' interviews and by material in the notebooks, she believed my project was sound and necessary. After my Ann Rutledge lecture was publicized in the East, Mrs. Dall defended my use of this personal history. In an article for the *New York Times* in December of 1866, she said, "We must trust Mr. Herndon because Abraham Lincoln trusted him." In a second, longer essay in the *Atlantic Monthly* in April of 1867, Mrs. Dall again defended me and my biographical project, asserting that "this nation owes to Herndon a great debt for first bending Lincoln's mind to the subject of slavery."

"A bit overstated," I told Anna about that sentence on slavery.

"You deserved her overstatement after she was snooping in your papers," Anna said.

"I told her she could look through the interviews. I'd forgotten the notebooks were in with my notes."

"How could you forget? You never allowed me to read those notebooks."

"Because some of the material there is not fit now for a woman's eyes."

"But you left the notebooks where **that** woman could see the material. Is it because she's more educated than your wife? Or because she shares each and every one of your beliefs and unbeliefs?"

"It was an accident, Anna."

"Perhaps, but first you invite that woman to stay in our home without asking me, then you go off to the office and leave me alone with a person I don't know, and then I'm the one who has to take the notebooks away from her. All for what? Some future recognition in the East?"

"Mrs. Dall will help me get the biography published."

"Only if you write it."

"You said I should."

"Now I'm not so certain it's worth your time if we will be subjected to the scorn your last lecture caused. Even the children hear 'Billy Betrayer.' You've let your practice languish since Mr. Lincoln's death, and we have nothing but debt to show for your researches. You received nothing from the lectures except insults."

I did not argue further with Anna at the time because I knew that Mrs. Dall was particularly nettlesome to my wife, but this conversation about our guest does indicate friction about my biography. Marymax would have helped me turn my fragmentary interview notes into sentences and paragraphs. She knew my hand and would give a hand because she shared my political sympathies and was fond of Lincoln who always treated her kindly when she came by the office. He called her "Millie" to rhyme, I suppose, with Billy, and would joke with her about having to listen to all of "Billy Book's ideas" just about every time she visited.

"But Mr. Lincoln," Marymax would say, "I read the books and give him the ideas in short form."

"Waal, Millie, could you make them forms shorter because when the ideas get over here to the office they get stretched out something fierce."

"I'll have him tell you about short stories by Edgar Allan Poe."

"I read his poems and some of his stories, but he uses a lot of long words."

"I will start embroidering his short words on pillows, Mr. Lincoln. William can bring you a pillow when he feels you need a new idea."

"Your husband is always saying I need new ideas, but what I really need is one of them pillows for my sofa, so I can sleep through his long ideas."

After several of these exchanges, Marymax asked me, "Is Mr. Lincoln really joking about your long ideas?"

"I assume so and joke back about his long stories. You do just fine."

"But I would not like it if he was being sarcastic about you."

"Lincoln thinks of himself as a peacemaker. Jokes and stories are sometimes his way of 'peacefully' instructing or criticizing. You have to remember he's the 'hoss' here."

Anna had never met the joking Lincoln. She was more prickly than Marymax and might have argued about my boss as the 'hoss.' It is easy for me to imagine Anna saying, "It seems like he's the rider and you're the colt." The daughter of Major George Miles, red-haired Anna was the belle of Petersburg and had spent a winter in Washington with family friends who were "in society." As a girl, Anna had the city experience that Mary Todd as a woman drove her husband toward. Eighteen years Anna's senior, with six children at home, I was no prize for the beautiful Miss Miles. Looking back now, I see that I was like Lincoln's father after Lincoln's mother died and a desperate Thomas proposed to Sarah Bush Johnston that they join households. I could promise Anna more than a log cabin, but she was not to be swept off her feet. To this ardent Democrat, my being the law partner of the Republican President Abraham Lincoln was not an advantage. But I was able to use my association with the president when courting Anna. One reason for my visit to the White House in 1862 was to secure an appointment for Anna's brother-in-law, Charles Chatterton, as an inducement for her to marry me. I also promised Anna that I would give up alcohol, and I joined the temperance organization Order of Good Templars.

With my persistence and the encouragement of her family, Anna finally surrendered and we were married in July of 1862. She moved into the house at First and Jefferson and immediately began improving the old manse—new wallpaper and curtains, shrubs and flowers. People used to walk by the house just to admire her roses. Maybe the physical changes came too soon and too fast after Mary's death, for my children never responded to Anna as we hoped. They refused to call her "Mother," and the older ones resisted a stepmother so close to their own ages. Anna was twenty-five when she came to Springfield; Nathaniel was twenty-one and Annie nineteen. Of the six, only "baby" Mary, who was six when I married Anna, grew close to her. When Anna gave birth to Nina in 1865, Mary was, in Anna's mind, Nina's "older sister" while the other children were half-sisters or half-brothers. Annie was, perhaps predictably, the most troubled by a stepmother named Anna. "If a young man comes courting," Annie asked me, "should I ask this old maid her advice?" "Twenty-five is not an 'old maid,' not any more," I said. "No? Then why didn't she find someone who wasn't an old man to marry?" If the fire ever went out in the stove, we could always rub Anna and Annie together to restart it.

Discussing Mrs. Dall in 1866, Anna was right about our financial situation. There were many mouths to feed. But after Lincoln left for the White House and my Mary died, I lost much of my interest in the practice of law. The office was lonely, the cases seemed trivial, the war dominated my attention. I had called for it, but it was going badly, the wounded and maimed were coming back to Springfield, and Lincoln was being assailed week after week by my antiwar brother and other Copperheads. I did take on a junior partner, Charles Zane, but our association was unprofitable for both of us. Lincoln's death further diminished my interest in fellow citizens' squabbles over property lines and runaway hogs. Lincoln became my mission. Although I could not be him, my biography could be like him: forthright, frank, true, plainspoken, maybe even somewhat improper. But after my Ann Rutledge lecture, many residents of Springfield lost trust in the man who bit Lincoln's back. And I took time away from the practice while I was doing my interviews and reading documents for my biography. There were travel expenses, clerical expenses, and at times I was forced to pay informants for their cooperation. I had to pay for notices in Illinois papers requesting information from anyone who knew Lincoln. Fearing the loss by fire of my notes, I had everything (except for the black notebooks) copied in the good round hand of John Spooner and bound in three leather volumes each about the size of Webster's dictionary. These volumes I called "The Lincoln Record." Adding up all of my expenses after my talk with Anna, I found that I had spent $1,536 on the project, thirty-six more dollars than the governor of Illinois earned in a year.

In early 1867, I proposed a fifth lecture—on Lincoln's childhood. This would have been the first chapter of my biography, but I did not have the information I needed about his Kentucky years, and I could not spare the time or expense to do more research away from home. I never wrote the lecture and thus did not truly start the biography. I owed it to Lincoln and to America, but neither altruism nor selfishness could motivate me. The biography was the only thing I wanted to do, and yet I could not do it. Throughout 1867 I forced myself to write wills and briefs, and I answered numerous letters from persons who inquired about Lincoln, but I could not begin the biography. I once told a friend that I knew Lincoln better than he knew himself, and I still felt that way about some of his silent places. Lincoln kept his depths secret from others and, I sometimes thought, from himself. Although he analyzed with great precision the world around him, he sometimes resisted analyzing—or intuiting—himself. Over the years, he gave me hints about his smiling mournfulness, and yet I was as wordless as the morning that James Plumley woke me to stammer that Lincoln had been shot. Down at the telegraph office that morning, I wanted to comfort the people who gathered there. But my Ann Rutledge lecture offended and alienated many of those same people, and I still was not able to write up my ideas about Lincoln's melancholia. How, I wondered, could this man so subject to sadness have written his Gettysburg Address in the midst of such death and destruction? Here I sit in a comfortable home surrounded by healthy, lively children and cannot begin a life as heroic as the forefathers Lincoln called upon that day.

I had fallen into one of Lincoln's hypos. I could not blame it on the death of a loved one such as Ann Rutledge, though Marymax was still often on my mind. I could not blame it on an unhappy marriage, for levelheaded Anna was nothing like bullheaded Mary Todd. In some ways, Anna was more like the longheaded Lincoln in her common sense. I sometimes believed that Lincoln never could overcome his fear that he was the illegitimate son of Nancy Hanks, but I was sure of my parents. More than ever, I needed to talk with my mentor. To me and others who studied in his office, his advice was always the same and simple: "Work and keep working." I kept thinking but could not work, could not act upon my desire. Desperate to resolve my hypo, I wondered what he would say if I could summon him like the ghost of Hamlet's assassinated father. I wrote out the following dialogue with the hope that imagining Lincoln's voice would help me begin his truthful biography:

"So, Mr. Lincoln, is there an afterlife?"

"No, Billy, just the lives who come along after us. I worried this to a nub as a boy. Kentucky was so far from any heaven I heard tell about, I reckoned it didn't exist. That made me sad, and I expect I never got over that feeling. But I figure it's made folks sad since they first started digging graves. Maybe that's why I loved old Byron. He had that feeling and still managed some greatness in his life."

"Do you mean the hypo is the natural state of mortal humans, and any happiness we have is a temporary change from our natural condition?"

"Not the natural state. Just the state of humans who observe carefully and think clearly."

"But we've shared this infidel skepticism since we met, Mr. Lincoln. Why am I afflicted by this hypo now?"

"Forget that Spencer feller and his 'causative.' A hypo don't need a cause that you or anyone else can analyze. I've had it strike me in the middle of a summation. It can pass just as quick telling a joke or a story."

"I'm no good at telling jokes and stories. I have to have a reason. My life's work—my Lincoln-like ambition—is to write this biography, and yet I cannot."

"Maybe your ambition is to be famous, like Robert said."

"You won't believe this, but I want to contribute to history what I know of science and politics and your exemplary life. If I could write it, I would be willing to publish it under another person's name."

"Maybe you shoot too high, fear the book will fail to reach up to your expectations."

"Or yours."

"Remember what I said about biographies. Booksellers ought to bind up some blank pages, and then every man could write the biography he wanted or needed."

"That was just a joke, Mr. Lincoln. I want to fill the blank pages with the truth."

"Yer truth is going to look like resentment or envy to some folks."

"I know about that. I have the will to oppose them but no passion, no vim. My blood seems to be moving as slow as yours. I've even started to walk like you, clumping along, not looking where I'm going. What could have cored me out like this?"

"Waal, Billy, don't never underestimate the hypotizing power of guilt. It married me off to Mary Todd. Remember what's in those notebooks."

I did not need Lincoln's ghost to remind me what was in the notebooks, but back then, so soon after his death, I knew I could not face down my guilt if I used some of that notebook material about my friend, not even if a story was instructive like the one about his drinking. I was not drinking when trying to start the biography, and yet I felt as if every day was the morning after. Barely able to walk to the office, unable to move the pen across the page, I often recalled Lincoln's remark that I was "too rampant and spontaneous." Not in those first months of 1867.

PART THREE

CHAPTER NINE

In the spring of 1867, my father, shortly before his death, deeded to me a farm of nearly six hundred acres along the Sangamon River. This gift changed my life and affected my writing right up to the present. Although my father and I differed over politics, particularly slavery, I and not Elliott had been his lawyer, and the war settled some of those old arguments. With his grandchildren, my father had no conflicts and loved them with none of the reserve I felt after returning from college. The farm, he made it clear, was primarily for them. "You and Elliott have made a comfortable living from the law," he told me on the day of the bequest, "but you can't pass on your law books the way you can acreage. If you get all your girls married off, Natty and Leigh can eventually take over the place."

My mother told me that Elliott had tried to talk my father out of the bequest. After my father's burial, I confronted Elliott at the cemetery to ask him why. He could not run away. Anna tugged at me, tried to remove me from Elliott's path, but I shook off her hand.

"You received a farm, too, Elliott. Why did you try to deny me?"

"Because you betrayed the Herndon family."

"Democrat, Republican, it is only politics. The labels will change. Blood will not."

"For you, it was not only politics. You sat in judgment of us. You wanted the world to believe you and your Lincoln were morally superior to us."

Anna tugged again and said, "William, let him pass. He is crazy with grieving."

"And I am aggrieved," I said to her and to Elliott. "Are you my brother, Elliott?"

"Are you the Herndon who is giving lectures that claim you—you—are even more morally upright than your partner? Your egoism offends anyone named Herndon, anyone but you."

With that Elliott raised a crutch to push me out of the way. Anna pulled me in the same direction, and my brother hobbled past.

"Let him go, William," Anna said. "His soul is crippled by rage and envy."

"But his charges?"

"Elliott is childless. He understands nothing about being a father, only a son."

"I never meant to insult my father with my political loyalties."

"I know. Remember, you are married to a Democrat."

"You're remarkably tolerant for one. Perhaps Elliott will insult you for moral tolerance next."

"From Elliott, I can run away. Unlike you who must run fast toward every possible conflict."

"If the conflict is moral, yes. If the conflict is over truth or justice, yes, I admit it."

"You see, Elliott may be partly right. Not even Lincoln ran toward every conflict."

"He had the nation on his back. At least he didn't run away. Elliott can never forgive him for emancipating the slaves."

Anna squeezed my arm, her signal not to take seriously what she would say next.

"Elliott should, I have."

"You had to, or you'd be running away from conflict with your morally pure husband every day."

Anna squeezed my arm again and said, "So maybe you, not Mary Todd, were the reason Mr. Lincoln spent so much time on the circuit."

"Lincoln loved to settle arguments in court but loved even more to stir them up in the office. He initiated most of the 'conflicts.' He knew I'd always rise to the bait. At home, Mary Todd started and ended the conflicts, with her broomstick or a block of wood if necessary."

Though tainted by Elliott's opposition, the farm was beautiful, sitting above the Sangamon six miles from Springfield. After my father's death, I used to go out there to talk with the tenant, enjoy the view of the river, and let the nature I loved as a youth renew my spirits. The river was not sublime like Niagara Falls, but there was something elegant in its bends and soothing in its slow movement. Before Lincoln was killed, my passions were positive. I worked **for** changes in society. I was frustrated by opposition parties, but my Emersonian optimism kept me "for." Since his death, my passions have been **against** what others wanted to do with Lincoln and wanted to do to me. In this regard, Anna was right. The land was not against me. I did not have to run to any conflict. Lincoln ran and ran and ran for offices. He once joked that he was so slow-moving because he was always tired from running. On the farm, I'd sit still and let the river run. It calmed me like Anna's hand on my arm. Some Sundays she and the younger children would go out with me, Baby Mary (now eleven) would chase around the chickens and scout for eggs, and we would have a picnic.

One such Sunday in August, I said to Anna, "Let's move out here."

The always cautious Anna asked, "What do you know about farming?"

"About as much as I knew about law or politics or Lincoln before I began studying them. Books, Anna. I've been reading the most recent books on horticulture. We could put this place on a scientific footing. Do planting on the slopes as it should be done. Grow things other farmers don't know how to. Put in some orchards. Use the railroads that moved troops to move our products to Chicago and even to the East."

"What about Mary's schooling?"

"We'll keep the house in town and live there during the school year. I'd be back and forth during those months, and we'd all live out here in the summer when the children can help with the work. Natty, Annie, and Beverly need jobs. You can find chores for Mary and little Nina to keep them out of your hair."

"And your law practice?"

"I'll work at it six months a year when the farm is dormant."

Later, not in this first conversation, she asked me about the biography. I thought that being away from the distractions of Springfield—the parade of twenty-dollar clients, running back and forth to the courthouse, the visitors seeking information about Lincoln, the daily correspondence, neighbors shunning me—would allow me to settle down and finally write the book that was my mission. Although Lincoln was a public man—lawyer, politician, and storyteller—he could be and often was remote, detached. Some days we would pass each other in the street, and he would not acknowledge me. This I understood, but he also could be detached from other friends and clients. His retreat was inside his skull. My retreat would be outside Springfield. After I finish my biography, I thought, I will ruminate like my cattle and perhaps write an eclogue—in English, my Latin being limited to legal phrases. The intellectual force I had always wanted would have the time and space to accumulate on the farm and could be exerted from afar, if six miles from the nearest post office is afar. Lincoln's life would be my lever. I had not been able to tilt him very far toward my positions, but I hoped my biography would lift readers with the example of Lincoln's character and would be a model of a new scientific biography. But, most importantly as my father said, the farm would give my family some security when I passed on. This latter argument for moving was persuasive for Anna, who also wanted, I believe, to get away from the enmity some of our neighbors and former friends had shown us since my Ann Rutledge lecture. I knew what Lincoln would have said about farming and what Thoreau did say about a farm: "That it makes but little difference whether you are committed to a farm or the county jail." But I still believed in his—and my earlier—teacher Emerson, who said in "Nature," "The health of the eye seems to demand a horizon. We are never tired, so long as we can see far enough." The farmhouse sat up on the Chinkapin Ridge where we could see up and down the river, so I renamed our second home "Fairview."

In the spring of 1868, we continued growing mostly corn but also planted five hundred grape vines along with four hundred apple, cherry and pear trees as a future investment. We had sixty cattle, one hundred or more hogs, and I bought twelve horses for plowing and Sunday riding. Natty cared no more for farm work than young Lincoln had, but the older girls pitched in to help Anna with a kitchen garden that grew more than even nine Herndons could eat. We had a dog for the first time, and Leigh became our resident horseman who tried to interest the girls in riding. "They are big ugly plow horses," they would complain to him. "We want delicate little mares." At least the horses were happy, for they had Sundays off. I was busier than I planned and had little chance to work on the biography. After the harvest I had to split time between the farm and the work that had accumulated at the office, and again the biography languished. I was in good spirits, had my old youthful enthusiasm, my Springfield hypo had disappeared, but I just did not have time to organize into an appropriate structure all the materials on Lincoln that I owned. My "scientific" ambition frustrated me. I could have written a chronological narrative of Lincoln's life, but how to come at that life from environmental, neurological, and psychological perspectives? That was the problem I could not seem to solve. I wanted a book like *Walden*. Not in what it told about the author but how it told the life of its subject—the pond—from multiple angles.

That summer crop prices started falling, and the Midwest, if not the entire country, entered a period of depression. Between 1868 and 1872 the price of corn in the Chicago grain markets fell by 50 percent. To buy a pair of boots, I had to grow fifty bushels or an acre of corn. Our long-term investment in fruit trees and vines had no chance. We would need to grow more corn for less money. Unable to afford all the day laborers the tenant used, Natty, Leigh, and I had to do much of the physical labor, which left me no energy to write and little time to spend at the office. I tried to borrow money to see us through this depressed period, but land prices were down and no bank would give me a loan. I took out a mortgage on the house in Springfield and sold off much of my library, at the time the most extensive in Springfield. Though not affecting the content of my biography, the loss of my books reminded me that I had not written my own. That fall I also lost Natty. He was a strapping young man, good with animals, could do large sums in his head, and had his mother's sweet spirit, but after her death I had not managed to send him to school, as my father did me, as Lincoln did Robert. Natty showed no interest in the law and could talk only of Chicago, where some of his friends had found jobs.

"Your grandfather wanted you and your brother and sisters to have this farm some day," I told Natty when he said he was leaving.

"There are too many of us. Who knows when my sisters will find husbands. If Leigh and I marry and have children, we will all starve."

"If all the young men move to Chicago, no one will grow food and they will starve there."

"You believe there is dignity in farming. I see only brutality. And fated failure. The secessionists lost the war because they lived like us, growing things. The North won by making things. That's the future, father."

How could I deny Natty? Lincoln left his father and moved on to city life. I rebelled against my father and then accepted the farm as a Herndon future. Already it was losing money and now its proposed inheritor. I would have to do more of the labor that Natty had performed or find men I could afford. There were men without jobs in Springfield, hanging about the streets and saloons. But many of them had lost a leg or their wits or their will in the war. Others refused to pick up a shovel again after digging trenches or graves. I often wondered what Lincoln would have said to these veterans if he had returned to Lincoln and Herndon. His jokes and stories might not entertain men who still wore scraps of blue.

Natty mentioned "fate," but what happened to the Herndons out on the farm was not fate. No, as we would learn in the coming years we were the victims of circumstances and conditions, of politics and economics that were like the iron rails of fate. In fact, the iron rails of the railroad were our "fate." Like so many other small farmers, we came to understand the meaning of the new phrase "railroaded." Back in my youth, I had wanted to be an intellectual force, to move people to liberation. In my middle age, I learned how financial forces could move me to desperation.

CHAPTER TEN

That winter after Natty left, Ward Hill Lamon paid me a surprise visit out at the farm. I knew Lamon from the days when he rode the circuit with Lincoln, and I had little respect for this abolitionist hater best known for drinking large amounts of whiskey and singing Southern songs. While he was marshal of the District of Columbia, he was Lincoln's unofficial bodyguard but was absent the night the president was shot. Back now in Illinois, Lamon affected an Eastern style with his oily tousled hair and walrus mustaches, which, though impressive, did not wholly distract attention from his jowls and heavy paunch. Although he had never been wounded to my knowledge, he carried a cane. He could have carried a parasol just as well, for I never saw him use the cane. I had not seen "Hill," as he was called, for many years, but he treated me like a familiar country cousin when he found me in my work clothes in the barn.

"So, Billy boy," he said while shaking hands and looking at my muddy boots, "you have left the profession of the law and become a gentleman farmer."

"A noble Jeffersonian citizen."

"I never thought you'd get ahead of old Ward."

"As big as you've gotten, Hill, just about anybody with two feet could get ahead of you."

I did not mention the cane.

"You know what I mean, Billy. You've been traveling the rutted roads and poking under the bushes, charming Abe's stepmother, talking to all the old toothless men up in New Salem."

"For my biography, you mean?"

"Your biography. How far along are you on that? I heard you ran into some grapeshot over one of your lectures."

"I work on it when I have time. Did you come out here to contribute a recollection?"

"Ah, no, you see I've been wanting to write a biography of my own capitalizing, so to speak, on my intimate knowledge of Honest Abe, my esteemed opponent out on the circuit. But since you've already done a full bushel of the research, I thought we might get together on this project and hurry it up before everyone forgets old Abe. There's money to be made, Billy. Look how much success that preacher Holland had by turning Abe into a miracle man."

My proposed collaboration with young Hart petered out after Holland published his book, but I told Lamon collaboration was a possibility, though I did not believe the blowhard could or would write a biography. If he did, it would be years in the making. I needed money now. We talked some more about how a collaboration might work, and I told him about my "Lincoln Record." When he realized all my research was clearly copied and bound in three volumes, he was less interested in collaboration, which was exactly my intent. We met the next day in my office so he could examine the "Record." I could tell he was excited as he paged through the volumes. He tried not to show it, but "Hill" was no stone-faced Lincoln, and he offered then and there to buy the "Record." I told him I might part with it but would have to think about terms. Thus began a protracted negotiation by mail where Lamon could better hide his desire. I proposed to "lease" him the "Record" for a specific period of time—during which I believed Lamon would never write a book. But he stalled and prevaricated, crop prices kept going down, rail charges kept going up, and I ended up selling him the "Record" for

$4,000, which would get me through another year or possibly two at Fairview. I retained the original documents, but I knew that losing the easily read and well organized "Record" would set back my own biography. I did not need Lincoln's ghost to remind me of guilt, but I desperately needed the money. And even after Lamon paid me the $4,000, I did not believe he had the discipline or intelligence to write a book.

I was right about Lamon, but he was, in fact, ahead of me. During our negotiations, he contracted Chauncey Black to write the book using my "Record." Black was a strange choice, a Democrat and no Lincoln lover, but his father had been in the administration so Lamon figured he could "capitalize" on that. After Black began, he realized there were gaps in the "Record" he would have difficulty filling because he never met Lincoln. So in 1870 Lamon wrote to me, saying, "I want to possess myself of your mind in regard to Lincoln—your theories respecting disputed points and facts, and your plan or scheme of life, and the influence of particular incidents on his subsequent character." I felt like replying that although I sold my "Record" I was not a candidate for "possession" like a slave in the peculiar institution that Lamon used to support. I was torn. I hoped Black would not be able to write the book, but if he did manage he would be relying heavily on my interviews. I did not want false conclusions about Lincoln drawn from my notes, and I still felt guilty about letting the "Record" out of my hands, so I wrote letters about my informants and memoranda about Lincoln for Black. I also loaned Lamon one of my two black notebooks, but despite repeated requests he never returned it and I worried that he would use information in it.

Anna thought the correspondence a waste of my precious time.

"Lincoln would probably agree with you," I told her. "He'd call my cooperation 'damned fool altruism.'"

"It's not just altruism. You're not just helping another, you're hurting yourself, your own book."

"I haven't been able to write it. If it turns out I can't, I still want people to know the Lincoln I knew."

"Now Lamon, who also knew Lincoln, will get the credit."

"Some credit. Lamon and Black will never know everything I do about Lincoln's history. Their book, if it's ever published, will be the Introduction. Mine will be the Conclusion."

Lamon's *Life* did get published in 1872. I had warned Lamon that not all of the informants in my "Record" could be trusted, either because of personal grudges or dim memories, and I trusted Black would heed my warnings, but he used every bit of ugly rumor and malicious gossip he could find in the "Record" and attached my name to all of it. His portrait of Lincoln was so distorted and antagonistic that Lamon excised Black's last chapter before publication without informing him. Even so, the book had no balance between Lincoln's flaws and his sterling character. It was the book that some listeners to my lectures accused me of wanting to write, an atrocious assault, a betrayal by a man that Lincoln had helped. And a man that I had helped. Lamon made a convenience of "Billy boy," as he addressed me out on the farm. But he also threatened my own future authority with his mix of gossip and facts. Fortunately, I still had one of my two notebooks. Since Lamon and Black used nothing in the one I loaned him, maybe one of them lost it—and that's why Lamon would not return it.

Most offensive to reviewers and readers all over the nation—and even abroad—were Lamon's pages on Lincoln's religion or lack thereof. I was the source of those pages, and ghostwriter Black quoted me at length. Here is a small sample:

"While it is very clear that Mr. Lincoln was at all times an infidel in the orthodox meaning of the term, it is also very clear that he was not at all times equally willing that everybody should know it. He never offered to purge or recant; but he was a wily politician, and did not disdain to regulate his religious manifestations with some reference to his political interests. As he grew older, he grew more cautious; and as his New Salem associates, and the aggressive deists with whom he originally united at Springfield, gradually dispersed, or fell away from his side, he appreciated more and more keenly the violence and extent of the religious prejudices which freedom in discussion from his standpoint would be sure to arouse against him. He saw the immense and augmenting power of the churches, and in times past had practically felt it. The imputation of infidelity had seriously injured him in several of his earlier political contests; and, sobered by age and experience, he was resolved that that same imputation should injure him no more."

These sentences drew much of the reviewers' anger, for the passage claimed not only that Lincoln was an "Infidel" but was not honest in hiding that fact. The reviewers' grapeshot went over Lamon's head and struck me. The hypocrite and novelist Holland fired away from his redoubt as editor of the influential *Scribner's Monthly*. Holland dismissed the biography as a "national misfortune" and blamed me, who had given him two days of my time to answer questions about Lincoln. Naturally, the paid defenders of the faith added their choir of criticism. James A. Reed, pastor of Springfield's First Presbyterian Church, gave a lecture on "The Later Life and Religious Sentiments of Abraham Lincoln" attacking the biography and me, a lecture that Holland printed in his magazine. Black wrote to me, explaining Reed's accusation: "You, being an infidel and therefore an immoral man yourself, have resorted to the basest means of proving that Mr. Lincoln was like you."

The farm exhausted me, but it was peaceful next to the Sangamon. I had fences but no walls, so poison could seep through from Springfield, Chicago, and any Eastern city large enough to have a newspaper. Again I was angry and ready to run "toward" and go "against." Though Black was not sincerely interested in biographical accuracy, he did want to sell books, so he suggested I write a lecture replying to Reed and deliver it right here in Springfield. I told Anna about Black's suggestion. After reminding me of the perils of altruism, she surprised me.

"I think you should," she said.

"We suffered from my Ann Rutledge lecture," I said, the voice of caution for once.

"It's different this time, William. Then they accused you of impropriety. This time they are accusing you of immorality."

"Elliott accuses me of moral pride, the clergy accuse me of moral turpitude."

"They say you are inventing as Holland did," she reminded me.

"But is a lecture the best response?"

"It will give you a chance to reply to all those who shunned us for the other lecture."

Anna's "us" explained one reason why she was now in favor of running toward conflict.

"This one would prove Lincoln an Infidel," I warned her.

"I live with one. Not all Infidels are damned forever. I have hope for you yet. But if you give the lecture, tell them everything you know. You still have your black notebooks."

"One of them. Lamon refuses to return the one I loaned him."

"Use it. Use everything. Put an end to these accusations. They distract you from more important work."

"I don't need everything, Anna. I'm still a lawyer. I can demonstrate Reed's inaccuracies and fallacies without using new information. I want to save the notebook for my own biography, if we ever get more than thirty cents a bushel for our corn."

I gave the lecture in December of 1873. Anna and my three oldest children were sitting in the front row for support. I was not the hound this time. I was the enraged bear, Reed was the little dog, and I shook the falsehoods out of him, impeached his "witnesses," and tossed in some of Lincoln's scoffing comments about "revealed truth." My last lines summed up my intent: to "put a stop to romantic biographies. Now let it be written in history and on Mr. Lincoln's tomb—'He died an unbeliever.'" The Herndons applauded but behind them many in the audience hissed or shouted, preparing all the Herndons for the response outside of Springfield. The broadside of my lecture was reprinted in cities all over the United States. The headline in the *New York Herald* summed up the judgment in almost all of the papers: "JUDAS IN SPRINGFIELD." I anticipated what the reception would be, and I refused to respond. I could not confront all my accusers as I could the Reverend Reed or Elliott or, in an earlier day, as Lincoln wrassled someone who insulted him or staged public debates with Douglas. Now conflicts were in writing—letters, papers, magazines, books. There was still oral argument in the courtroom, but we were far from Speed's dormitory where we argued politics and religion face to face deep into the night. The scores of newspapers who mocked me had thousands of words and maybe millions of readers. I had the words of my informants and of Lincoln. One day I would have my revenge on the philistines and liars. I vowed I would write out the last word on Lincoln and the word of God in a biography that would be sold in every city and town with a newspaper.

But when the *Illinois State Journal* persuaded Mary Todd Lincoln to call me a liar, I could not stay silent. Mary Todd said in an interview that she never had a conversation with me at the Saint Nicholas Hotel where she confessed Lincoln "was not a technical Christian." Anna urged me to respond to this blatant lie.

"You're as bad as Mary Todd," I joked with Anna, "pushing your husband to do something he doesn't want to do."

"You're as bad as Mary," Anna replied, "lying to my face about what I know you want to do."

"It would make us even more enemies in town."

"You may be wrong about that. Mrs. Lincoln was disliked by many women in Springfield for her 'aristocratic' airs and temper tantrums. Perhaps you will regain their husbands as clients if you embarrass her. Besides, I do not want to have a husband who is a 'liar.' "

"Honest Anna," I said.

"Honest Abe was worth imitating when he wasn't wrong about politics."

I had the letter from Mary Todd agreeing to the interview, and I had my notes, and both were published in newspapers and in a broadside in early 1874. Lincoln had allowed his wife to be the hound at his ass. To show her as an outright liar was long-delayed justice for me—and for my dead friend. When Mary Todd first came to Springfield, she was an intelligent and educated woman, better schooled than either her husband or me. Her learned ambition combined with Lincoln's natural ambition, and may even have spilled over toward me. I wondered if Mary's Lincoln had told me about Raymond's rise down in New Orleans to encourage his junior partner to be more ambitious, more interested in adding clients than in adding books to our office library. But Mary Todd's ambition crazed her like Lady Macbeth, maybe not coincidentally Lincoln's favorite Shakespeare play. Some months after I exposed her lie, Mrs. Lincoln was committed to an asylum by Robert. I took no pleasure in the news because I often felt like another Shakespeare character, the dithering Hamlet who cannot do right by his father and who suffers both the world's "contumely" and "the slings and arrows of outrageous fortune." I did not want to murder anyone, just write my biography, but the banks where I applied for loans that would give me some relief from labor were Polonius: "borrowing dulls the edge of husbandry."

Now I feel free to reveal the notebook material that Anna wanted me to use when under attack by the rampant Christians and Mary. Lincoln's reliance on his own perceptions and his natural suspicion of anyone claiming a monopoly on truth would have been enough, along with his reading of Paine, to make the youth a skeptic, but his journey out of the backwoods to New Orleans confirmed his freethinking position. It did not change as long as I knew him. I wrote his private secretary, John Nicolay, to ask if Lincoln's skepticism shifted in the White House, and Nicolay thought not.

After some client would appeal to divine intervention or bless Lincoln for his help on a case, he would wait to hear footsteps go down the stairs and then say something scoffing like "More voodoo, Billy" or "Get out the drums" and pitch into this New Orleans story with the same enthusiasm he showed for Raymond's rise as a wood merchant. Lincoln and Gentry went to a place called Congo Square on Sundays. It was the Negro servants'—and maybe some slaves'—day off, and they gathered in the park to play their drums and dance. Lincoln had never seen anything like it.

"You should have seen the drums, Billy. These ain't those little rat-a-tatters soldiers step to. Some were four feet tall, as big around as beer barrels and painted all different colors. There was a line of them, maybe a dozen drums of different sizes, and men stripped to the waist thumping on them with both hands. There was no leader, but them drummers somehow knew how to keep together even though they were half dancing while beating the skins. Men and women were dancing on the grass in front of them, no dance like I could have imagined down in Kentucky. They twisted up their bodies like circus performers and leaped around like scared cats. They were chanting in some African language Raymond couldn't understand."

"This was after church, I guess," I said, meaning to josh Lincoln about not attending, but he missed my intent.

"This was their church and religion, Raymond told us, that voodoo slaves had brung up from Haiti. All by word of mouth, no books, gods and goddesses by the dozens, Raymond said. Right thar was when I realized the Ten Commandments were just a set of laws made up by Moses to rule the drummers and dancers. The gospels are the revised code. Some good ethics and some bad laws in them old holy books, but a body'd need to be a fool to believe jest one God came down to earth and got Joseph's Mary with child."

"I guess you didn't join in."

"You know I can't dance, Billy, and I can't believe Americans are still singing hymns about events that might have happened two thousand years ago and a heap more than two thousand miles away. If slavery was abolished and those dancers come up north, the Methodists and Baptists would go out of business."

Up in New Salem there were many Protestant sects with small but fervently held differences in doctrine. In New Orleans, Lincoln witnessed large differences, which confirmed his skepticism of Christianity as the one true religion. He saw priests and nuns in robes and a cathedral with stained glass that would have been an abomination to Calvinists worshipping in log cabins. Raymond pointed out a synagogue. Gentry treated it like a zoo. He asked Raymond if they could go in and "see some real live Jews." No, but he did take them into a Catholic church. The priest might as well have been speaking Hebrew as Latin because none of the Kaintucks could understand a word. Lincoln realized that all who worshipped did so in different ways to different gods. He told me, "the drumbeat might be the same, but the dancers are all moving on their own, Protestants and Catholics and Infidels. After concluding this, I couldn't sit in a pew or listen to any Christian preacher."

"Haven't I seen you come out of First Presbyterian with Mary?" I asked.

"I go once in a great while to please her and my constituents. It's a good cool place on a hot summer day."

Though not intuitive about individuals, Lincoln did sense about religion what scholars later in this century would demonstrate with their "Higher Criticism" of the Bible—that it was a historical document like other ancient documents, that it was one of many texts claiming to be sacred, that religions were constructed by cultures, some very different from

Kentucky. Back there in New Salem reading Paine, Lincoln was your village atheist, maybe to shock like some of his stories did. But in New Orleans his perception was more profound. He realized not just that the Bible and Christianity were not rational but that all religions had their source in irrationality.

As far as I could tell, poor Lincoln had the worst of unbelief and belief: he could not believe in a rescuing afterlife but did believe that some force mysteriously fated common events. More for the sake of his listeners than for himself, Lincoln during the war often pleaded in his speeches for strength from a providential God he did not believe in. During his administration, "In God We Trust" started appearing on currency. Observers such as Holland and the Reverend Reed explained Lincoln's success as part divine grace. I knew better—about Lincoln, about the war—and I vowed back then that Lincoln's power as a perceiving, thinking biological "organism," a natural and rational man, would receive the credit it and he deserved when I could manage to write my damned biography. "Damned" because composing it frustrated me, and "damned" because I knew that is what it—and I—would be called when it was published.

Chapter Eleven

The attacks by Christians who were now feeling the pinch of Darwin, as well as Spencer, continued long after my "Judas" lecture, so I wrote a few short essays for various Free Thought publications around the country defending my Infidelism and documenting Lincoln's. Given the vitriol of the Baptists and Methodists, you would think I was a literal Infidel, a Mohammedan that the Crusaders needed to drive from Illinois. In my essays I counterattacked by proposing civil marriages and easy divorces to break the monopoly of the churches on marriages. These proposals were in line with my earlier support for women's rights because women were the primary victims of the divorce laws. Too often, the office of Lincoln and Herndon heard the stories of women assaulted by their husbands or slandered by other men, but it was difficult to get the women relief or compensation for all the labor they had contributed in the henhouse, dairy, kitchen, and sewing room. Not surprisingly, my proposals were unpopular and could never be legislated if women were not allowed to vote. About the only support I received was from Mrs. Dall, who wrote me several letters praising me for bringing the same attention to indentured women that I had to enslaved Negroes. Reading these letters, Anna softened her view of the "snooping" Mrs. Dall. "Maybe she will invite us to stay in her home in Boston," Anna said, "and I can tell her about wearing your old boots in the barn."

During the 1870s, it was economics, more than religion, that interfered with my biography. Nature did not betray my trust at Fairview. It was the trusts—the corporations and monopolies—that betrayed me and the bounty I could produce but not sell for a fair price. In politics, I favored the radical Reconstructionism of Grant, but I soon felt in my arthritic knees and aching shoulders the effects of electing this Republican war hero. Poverty and physical labor taught me that Lincoln's policy of protectionism from foreign imports continued by Grant protected only the interests of the big-money Eastern Republicans, especially the railroad price fixers and commodities manipulators. The small farmer and wage laborer who were central to the Republican platform in the 1850s were out of luck with Grant's crony criminals. In 1870 I gave a very well-attended lecture in Springfield where I admitted I was wrong to embrace Lincoln's policies on the central bank and the protective tariff. The tariff may have helped the North win the war, but afterward the only winners were the corporations and monopolists. Without competition from foreign-made goods, they could keep prices artificially high, and when one combine or trust destroyed internal competition, prices for American-made goods went even higher. My Spencer and his "survival of the fittest" had been kidnapped from biology and used to defend economic piracy.

Like any words by William Herndon, the economics lecture was picked up by newspapers in Illinois and around the country. Republican papers mocked me, of course. First Billy betrayed his friend the Republican Founder, next he betrayed the Founder's party. The person or legend of Lincoln was still so powerful that no reasoned objections to the policies he instituted could be spoken without that curse of "betrayal." Republicans believed Lincoln was a second savior. Religion wasn't politicized. Politics was religionized. Christianity had a monopoly on American thinking more powerful than any held by the money monopolists. My own thinking took a backward turn, a "causative" perspective. My commitment to a true life of Lincoln led to my alienation from my law practice and then to the Herndons' alienation from Springfield, which led to our retreat to the farm, which became unprofitable due to Lincoln's policies, which led me to sell my "Record" to Lamon, which caused me further alienation from the public and further delay in my life of Lincoln which was beginning to seem to me (and no doubt to Anna) like a curse, like Lincoln's "fate."

The summer of 1870 I had just enough cash to hire two Negroes to help chop corn. They had been slaves on a sugar plantation in Louisiana and turned up in Springfield on their way to Chicago. Somehow they knew I had been Lincoln's partner. They referred to him as "savior Abram," so there was no escaping religious veneration of the old Infidel. The Negroes' name was Top, brothers Richard and Robert, both in their midthirties it appeared. Richard did the speaking for both of them. "We both Top," he said, "but Robert don talk." I did not know if he disliked talking to white people or did not talk to anyone but his brother. Even Richard was hard to understand sometimes, but he understood what I asked him to do and relayed the instructions to Robert. They were good workers, adept with the sickle and used to the heat. They slept in the haymow as we had no quarters for them. I asked Richard to eat with us in the evening, but he pointed to his clothes and said, "They smell bad, boss." The Tops washed their one set of clothes on Sundays and hoped for sun.

I had defended several fugitive slaves, but Anna and the children had probably never spoken to Negroes. Mary Todd Lincoln kept Negro servants, but the Herndon women always did their own cooking and cleaning. My daughters said that was the reason I had so many daughters. Unfortunately, out at the farm there was little occasion for contact with the Tops, but we all shared a picnic dinner one Sunday evening when their clothes were clean and dry. I was the Herndon family spokesman. I asked Richard what they would do in Chicago since there was no cane or corn to harvest in the city. Robert surprised me by making a quick, sharp cutting motion. Richard laughed and said, "Plenty to kill up dere." I could see

Anna and the children who were listening were taken aback, so I quickly said, "You mean you'll work in the slaughter-houses?" Richard did not understand. "Butcher meat," I said. Robert nodded, and Richard added, "Must always be somepin for niggers to do in a city." Again my family was taken aback, for the children were forbidden to use "nigger."

"Well, up there," I said, "you won't have to sleep in a barn."

"Nah, Mr. Billy, up there we stack."

"Stack?"

"We live on top each other." Richard motioned with his hands, bottom to top, top to bottom, and laughed. "Have to pile up to keep warm at night."

To everyone's surprise, including Richard's, Robert spoke: "No, brother," he said, and held his hands side by side.

Richard laughed and said, "Robert ain do top and bottom unless he on . . ."

That was when I interrupted and asked Richard if they chose the name Top.

"Damn right," he said, and then quickly "pardon me, ladies."

Anna nodded to him, and Richard went on: "Slave name was Toppingham. I din't know to spell it. So we choose 'Top.' We the Top men."

At that, both Richard and Robert laughed, and who could deny them. But I feared they would be no better off on top of or next to each other in Chicago than here in my haymow. Natty found a job working on plank road construction but said he was lucky to get it because of all the white immi-grants. Negroes were emancipated, but Reconstruction was not working if their liberty led them to the slaughterhouses—of livestock and men—in Chicago.

By 1871 I could no longer pay my mortgage on the house in Springfield, it was foreclosed, and we moved to Fair-view full time. In 1872, I switched allegiance to the splinter Liberal Republican Party, but they failed to attract voters, so a year later I helped sponsor an independent, antimonopolist party. It also failed. My finances became more perilous during the Panic of 1873, and I deeded what was left of the farm to Anna to avoid foreclosure. I told her I hoped I could trust her not to run me off. "Those easy divorces you proposed aren't law yet, William," she said. "And Leigh can't do all the man's work alone." I have before me a copy of the Sangamon County Deed Record: seventy-eight acres, one house, one barn, twenty-five Berkshire hogs, one roan colt, one milk cow and calf, and a mule named Tom. That was what Fairview had been reduced to.

When we began farming, we had little to do with our neighbors. But the closer some of them got to us by buying our acres, the closer we got to them. I took notes on our conversations with the view of giving another lecture on the real lives of my contemporaries if my real life of Lincoln remained derailed by the fiasco with Ward Lamon. Young Patrick Moore was particularly friendly after he bought the last of my cattle. He occasionally stopped by with meat after he butchered a steer I had owned.

"Brought some Priscilla—or Fancy or Linda, I can't be sure—for you and the family, Mr. Herndon."

"Don't let the little ones hear you say that, Patrick, or they'll go to being vegetarians."

"Prices as low as they are in Chicago, it's better to feed the corn to the stock, eat the meat, and not get robbed by the railroads. Last time I shipped cattle up there, the stock-yard charged me twice as much for feed corn as what they'd paid two months before."

"We'd be better off making corn liquor."

I could see Patrick flush around his freckles, but he graciously let that remark pass. He found me passed out on the road from Springfield one night and brought me home in his wagon. After I was forced to give up the house in town, I also gave up temperance and too often put my cares to sleep in the bottle or beside the road.

"Tell me, Patrick. How did you do it, manage to prosper through these hard times?"

"You bought stock and invested in all your improvements at just the wrong time, Mr. Herndon. My father and I have been farming a long time, and we put money aside when we saw what was coming with the new Republicans. No offense, sir."

"Did you fight in the war, Patrick?"

"The Moores are all loyal Copperheads. My brother gave his life for your law partner."

"Still Democrats, then?"

"Yes, sir. I heard about your lecture on protection. Sounds like you're leaning our way now."

I was afraid to ask Patrick how he felt about slavery and Reconstruction. But he was right. I was leaning his way when not leaning against a bar. I was attending Grange meetings, and Anna sometimes went along because the Grangers were interested in the rights of farm wives as well as farmers. I listened to the complaints of other small farmers, too small like me to invest in the mechanical sowers and harvesters the families with larger farms could afford. I even read the local Democratic papers, including the one that used to be edited by my brother.

Anna said I ran to conflicts, but where would I run to confront the forces that ground down small farmers like me? I was used to word battles, up close or far away. The war between the trusts and individual citizens was so unbalanced that words in editorials and broadsides were obsolete, like bows and arrows. Only the numbers printed on greenbacks were weapons, and the monopolies held most of those. Farmers had food as a weapon, but it had to be sold every year if they were to survive. The capitalists could stockpile their money; it did not spoil like our produce. Rails were never ruined by too much or not enough rain. Steam engines might explode once in a while, but late snow or hail did not destroy them. I missed the old targets of my anger: townsmen who shunned me, writers like Holland whom I had met, Reverend Reed, even Mary Todd. They were alive and might register my response to them. The rails were inanimate and extended as far as I could see in any direction.

Thinking about the railroads, I remembered how impressed Lincoln was with the Pontchartrain railroad that he rode just after it opened during his second trip to New Orleans. The first railroad west of the Appalachians, it connected Lake Pontchartrain, where some passenger ships docked, to the port on the Mississippi. Although the rails were only five miles long, and the cars were drawn by horses, Lincoln thought it the height of land transport:

"No ruts, no mud, no stones, no broken axles, a smoother ride than a steamboat, Billy. No waves, no wakes. They even have men every quarter mile picking up the horseshit, so it's a sweet-smelling trip. It's mostly to move freight, but folks climb on just to ride on rails. Some of it is built up on swamp land, so it's straight and level as a billiard table, and cars roll along slick as balls on felt. It don't cost but twenty-five cents for a round trip. Soon they'll have steam engines dragging them cars, and then they'll be moving heavy loads back and forth just like on the rivers."

On that second trip, Lincoln also went downriver from the flatboat wharves to get a closer look at the coastal ships:

"Some of them ocean steamers make our riverboats look like flatboats. The stacks are taller than any tree you've seen. Shoot, the deck is up at tree top level from the water. None of them slap-water paddlewheels. Giant screws down below the surface move them ships through the waves. Their prows look like they could bust right through the Presbyterian church. I'm telling you, that port of New Orleans makes a Kaintuck proud to be an American."

"Who was loading and unloading the cargo?" I asked.

"I expect it was mostly slaves, but a lot of it was done with winches and such. Big old bales of cotton going out. And dry goods coming in from New York and Boston."

"Why don't those Americans down in New Orleans use the cotton to make clothes right there?"

"Maybe they can't train the Negroes. It's industry. The circle keeps both ends humming. But there is a one-way trade that was most amazing to me. Ice. One of them steamers was carrying nothing but ice packed in sawdust up in New England. You never seen men scamper like them unloading it, getting it transferred to New Orleans ice houses before that luxury turns into worthless water, which they got plenty of in Louisiana."

Back when I first heard Lincoln enthuse about new transport, I assumed it was just the country boy in the city. But one of the planks that drew Lincoln to the old Whig Party was its support of "internal improvements," which meant canals, harbors, bridges, and railroads. When he first ran for the Illinois House, he promised voters to make the Sangamon navigable. During his presidential campaign, he supported a transcontinental railroad. Lincoln was forward thinking, and one reason the North won the war was superior railroads, as well as manufacturing, but that little horseshit train he rode down in New Orleans became a monster after the war. Grand for corporations and industries but gobbling up small farmers.

Although 1874 was not a presidential election year, I was no longer "leaning," as Patrick put it. In October I wrote to the *Illinois State Register* denouncing "the corruptionists who congregate at the national capital, including the president himself" and urging citizens to vote for Democratic nominees across the state. Having been active in the founding of the Republican Party in Illinois, I felt regret and a little guilt, but "gimme" Grant was not Honest Abe.

"Now that I've converted you," Anna said after I announced myself as a Democrat, "you'll also give up writing all that Free Thought nonsense and start going to church with the girls and me."

"I can't afford to believe in Christianity," I told her, "because your God said to rest on the seventh day, but I can't or my Christian wife and children will starve."

"Maybe if you'd been like Moses and stuck to the law, you'd still be able to rest on Sundays."

"No, then I'd be working on my gospel of Lincoln."

"I will praise the Lord and Lincoln if that ever gets finished before end times."

Anna was good with needlework, both making clothes for the children and sticking pins in her husband. With no Lincoln around to tell stories and jokes, I had to depend on her wit, even if it was sometimes sharp. She never called me "Billy," but she often seemed older than me, not as craggy as old Abe but mature and wise beyond her years. The more we were isolated out on the farm, the better we got along, maybe because we had to pull together like Lincoln and Herndon. She was not the lady at home; I was not the gentleman at the office. We were woman and man, she with dirty hands from her garden, me with muddy boots from the fields. She was also a woman eighteen years younger than her husband. I would not want to challenge her to a wrassle out in the yard. She used to get the girls to arm wrestle on the kitchen table, but they soon gave up because no one could beat her. I didn't try. In the evenings we used one lantern and read to each other when the children were quiet. Like Lincoln, she was impatient with my poets and philosophers, and I would tolerate her fondness for Poe's stories in a volume that Mary 'had bought and the children had read. "Tolerate" because Poe's tales were even less likely than some of Lincoln's. Anna also read the Montgomery Ward catalogue and Grange pamphlets, though not aloud like Lincoln used to read the newspapers. From listening to other farm wives at the Grange, Anna was becoming more aware of women's labor.

"Why is it," she asked one day in the barn, "that it's always women who milk the cow?"

"Milk is women's specialty. Also it's easier than shoveling out this manure."

"But you do that once a day, and I have to squeeze old Alma here twice."

"Neighbors used to make fun of Lincoln because Mary made him milk the cow, but I guess nobody will see me. We can trade off, if you want."

We did, and Anna got very strong in her arms because she ended up shoveling manure into the wheelbarrow twice a day since she liked to keep a clean barn as well as house. Then she made Mary do the shoveling, and I was still milking the cow, so I told her I was not taking her to any more Grange meetings, to which she said she would have Leigh teach her how to ride our mule and go by herself. I could not let her have the last line, so I said, "I hope you will ride sidesaddle like the lady I married." But as Lincoln so often did, she topped me with, "Surely, William, because that's the way Jesus is pictured entering Jerusalem in my Bible."

Chapter Twelve

Anna and I sold some more acreage and limped along. Natty sent a little money from his job, Beverly married a man over in Menard County, and Lizzie made a few dollars helping out the Moores with their two small children. I gave up on practicing in Springfield and tried to pick up some clients in Petersburg. I hung about the courthouse, told Lincoln stories, and let people buy me drinks. I rarely found enough clients worth being away from the farm, so I jumped at the chance to make some new acquaintances and perhaps find some new clients when I was invited to address an "Old Settlers' Convention" by Milton Hay, who had read law with Lincoln.

The meeting was a late August barbecue where the mosquitoes, as usual, would probably be the best fed. I was happy to see women and men older than I, some of them true settlers like my father from the thirties, some their children. After Hay introduced me, I told the crowd of two hundred or so that I came to sod-busting late and was, therefore, right appreciative of the hardships pioneers had faced with wooden plows. I told them an old joke the womenfolk would appreciate—that Illinois was great for men and horses, hell on women and oxen. I remarked on the many changes in life the war had brought, and said that Lincoln and I were the "New Settlers," the city slickers who settled disputes rather than the land. I meant it as a joke to honor the labor of the true settlers, but I suppose I lacked Lincoln's humorous delivery. A man near the front stood up, raised the stump of his right arm, and hollered, "It cost me an arm for your Lincoln to settle that dispute with the South." I attempted to pacify the man who, upon closer inspection, also had a mangled ear. "I'm sure folks here appreciate your sacrifice," I said, "but remember that dispute cost Lincoln his life." "But none of his sons," a woman spoke from somewhere in the middle of the group. "He took two of my boys. And for what? We was better off before that war launched all the Irish and other immigrants into Illinois. There's a Catholic church now in Springfield. You walk down the streets over there and cain't hardly understand half the talk you hear. Only word that everybody knows is 'cash, cash, cash.'" More voices rose in a gabble, and Hay got up to quiet them, but the man with one arm hollered at him, "You're responsible, too, Milton, your nephew wrote down the orders that killed many a good man." Then a man who identified himself as a Methodist minister stood up and managed to settle down the "Old Settlers," but Hay and I left before the food was served.

I was never so happy to see a Christian minister. Some of those old folks were the Know Nothings that gained influence when the Whigs collapsed before the war, but they did know something about the damage the war had done to small communities, not just with men lost or, like the man with one arm, lost to labor, but with a way of life replaced. Trust and credit and barter were gone; manufacture, commerce, and greenbacks were in. Elliott had no practical excuse for similar attitudes, but, like me, the Old Settlers might not be able to make enough on their farms to buy the goods that were rapidly replacing homespun cloth and home-smoked bacon. I could not be angry at them and their resistance to the new America, but I still believed the war was just and necessary. I had to. Otherwise, I could not go on with my life of Lincoln. More and more, I felt, the kind of moral principle Lincoln represented was difficult to defend. Principal ruled, interest rates were high, and cash, as the woman said, was king. But on the long wagon ride home I was oddly happy. The road had been improved to reach the railhead, the brothers Top were in Chicago, and there was no stenographer to take down and circulate to the nation's newspapers the Old Settlers' attack on Billy and "his" war.

That winter, like the ones before, I was constantly down with influenza and afterward painful neuralgia that sometimes prevented me from doing my chores. That left Leigh the only man on the farm, and he was not much more robust than I. I rarely walked into Springfield, and most of my correspondents stopped writing to me, which saved on postage. But I was still Lincoln's Billy, good for an occasional taunting news story. A Kansas paper said I was a "pauper and common drunkard." Greeley's old paper, the *Tribune*, "reported" in September of 1877 that because of failing health I had attempted suicide by taking an overdose of laudanum. I had no money for newspapers, but Annie heard about this article and brought the issue home for me. Where was the outcry against "revealing" private "information" that was raised after my lecture on Ann Rutledge? I wasn't even dead yet. But I was Billy Herndon, not Abraham Lincoln, so anything could be written about me. Some newspapers were becoming fiction. Maybe Lincoln was right about "low lying." There was no forum for a response. The attack was personal, not political. And I was finding it more difficult to be righteously angry. So I just wrote a letter to the *Tribune* to say I never took laudanum, hoped "to live just one hundred years, and to do good to my fellowman to the end."

But William Herndon a suicide! Hamlet thought about it, and Lincoln may have considered it twice when he had his women troubles but not me. Injin Bill, Turkey Bill, Lincoln's Billy trying to kill himself? Yet there was truth to the paper's report that my health was failing. Not only my health. I had been failing for years, failing to keep up my law practice, failing to write my biography, failing at farming, failing again to write my biography, failing to discipline my drinking, failing to be the husband and father my family deserved. At this lowest point of my life I realized I was heading down to the life Lincoln had risen from. We intersected at the law office.

He rose higher as both character and statesman. I was going backward to the primitive labor and poverty he fled in Kentucky. And I couldn't blame the fate Lincoln believed in.

When I converted "failing" to flat-out "failure," I realized that Lincoln had also often been a failure on the way up. He was terribly disappointed after winning the debates against Douglas but losing the election in 1858. He used to tell friends, "I expect everyone to desert me except Billy." Lincoln moped around the office, kept asking me what he'd done wrong against Douglas, and figured his political career was finished. It was in that mood—the reverse of his earlier New Orleans enthusiasm—that he told me more about his second trip south in 1831.

"Offutt hired me, a man named Johnston, and cousin John Hanks to take some hogs down river. Offutt never built the boat, so we was delayed while John and I put one together. First day on the Sangamon we run aground on the New Salem dam and folks came out to laugh and holler. They was making fun of the rail-splitter, so I guess you'd call that raillery, wouldn't you?"

Like his Shakespeare and the dialect humorists he read, Lincoln loved puns, the worse the better. I told him not to derail his story.

"Down in Beardstown," he continued, "Johnston and Hanks went on a spree, and I nearly quit. John did quit in Saint Louis, leaving me and Johnston to shovel the hog shit off that boat. When we got to New Orleans, I depended on Offutt to sell his hogs. He was an experienced flatboater, but he was even more experienced as a carouser and drinker, so we got a low price. Came time to break up the boat, Offutt hated to sweat. When I got most of our wood in a pile, Offutt and I went to Raymond's house. I figured he'd be along the wharf and we'd get a Kaintuck price, but he warn't among the many clean-handed men that looked us over.

"When we got to his street," Lincoln told me, "his cottage was gone. So was the one next to it. A two-story house sat nice and new in the middle of the two lots. It sure wasn't carpentered out of beat-up flatboat wood either. 'Raymond is really coming up in the world,' I said to Offutt. I knocked on the front door, and a Negro man came after a while and opened it. I asked if Mr. Raymond was at home.

" 'He gone,' the Negro said.

" 'When will he be back?'

" 'He gone. This house belong to Mr. Colvin.'

" 'Do you know where I can find Mr. Raymond?'

" 'He gone.' "

Lincoln and Offutt asked around the wharves for Raymond and got the same answer. He was gone. They did no better on the lumber than on the hogs, though Lincoln said Offutt paid him well for getting the boat to New Orleans with the sail Lincoln rigged up. Lincoln stayed a week or more and hoped to run across Raymond but never did. "Just up and disappeared, Billy."

"Maybe he took his money and servants back up to our birth state where he is living high on those good Kaintuck hogs."

"I don't credit it. The way folks said 'gone,' I believe Raymond's business went under and he was gone underwater somewheres."

"Why do you think that?"

"The way folks shut their mouths after they said 'gone.' As if Raymond done something wrong and was punished for it. Like he was gone to hell."

"Maybe someone did wrong to Raymond. Maybe he was the victim of a crime."

"Could be, Billy, but from what we see of the law in here most folks are victims of crimes against themselves."

I was a little skeptical about Lincoln's conclusion. For him, failure was often accompanied by a helping of guilt. If you went wrong, you must have been guilty of something. If Douglas got more votes, Lincoln must have done something wrong. I might have agreed about the war: the rebels were wrong and got crushed. After the war I'd failed at many things, but I'd been crushed by the monopolies. My wrong:

inheriting a farm. Or maybe, far enough back, deciding to write the biography of Lincoln. In 1858, I reminded Lincoln he'd received more popular votes than Douglas and our Republicans were stronger in our canvass. But it was hard to pull Lincoln up out of a hypo because he had this history of failure. In New Salem, he and another man ran a store that failed and saddled Lincoln with debt he was still paying off when we were partners. His youthful investment in a steamboat failed. His horse and surveying tools were sold at auction to settle debts. Lincoln lost his first election in 1832, lost his first case in 1837, lost his first run for nomination for Congress in 1843. He could not persuade two women to marry him, and did not escape Mary Todd. He temporarily lost his mind after Ann Rutledge died and again before Mary Todd harnessed him. All these things creased and cursed him, but he kept plodding on with those long legs and big feet, hauling whatever guilt he felt behind him.

What was the origin of that will, what some called stubbornness, others called pride? What could I learn from my friend's persistence? The more I was worn down by farm labor, the more I believed the source was his physical stature and strength. Informants told me he could heave a small cannonball farther than any man. He survived the knock on his head when attacked on his first trip to New Orleans and a kick in the head from a mare when he was a boy. No matter what losses he suffered, he always occupied that six-foot, four-inch body that had been muscled and sinewed when young. At five feet and nine inches and with muscles trained by lifting Blackstone, I was failing at middle age to do the farm labor Lincoln hated as a youth. A decade after his death, I envied my friend's force. It, along with his will and mind, lifted him out of the fields. My will and mind were addled by drink and defeat. I could not even lift my pen to write the biography. Maybe Lincoln's sense of physical superiority got him killed when he went to Ford's Theatre without his bodyguard. My physical inferiority was killing me slowly on the farm in the 1870s.

CHAPTER THIRTEEN

I n January of 1880, to inaugurate the new decade, Anna suggested I look back through my interview notes and black notebook. She did not say we were desperate, but she did let on she fancied one of those new-fangled washing machines they were selling in Springfield. She hoped I would somehow finally compose the biography, write us out of poverty, and get her hands out of the washtubs.

"I don't need pure white hands," she said.

"What do you mean?" I asked.

"You don't look at women, William. I should be pleased. Some farmers' wives bleach their hands so others will believe they don't work in their gardens."

"This is what you notice when you go in to church?"

"Or when I have a few pennies to buy ribbons for the girls' hair."

Mary and Lizzie had found husbands without bleaching their hands. Their marriages were bright spots, even if I did have to usher them down the aisle of a church. They both wed railroad men, so their futures were probably secure, and I swallowed my denunciations of the rails for a few months. Anna was happy to have the girls out of the house. There was less wash but fewer hands. Leigh was still helping me and had built himself a little house down the road. Nina was fifteen, William ten, and Minnie five, so we still had five of us to feed and clothe, and two to send to school in Springfield. I was sixty-one and resigned that I was never going to be able to plant more corn no matter what the prices were. Looking again through my notebook and loose materials, some now ragged from being read and shuffled so often, I realized that it was not strength alone that saved Lincoln from his failures. It was honesty. He got the nickname "Honest Abe" from judging horse races up in New Salem. Honest about horses, he was usually honest with people. But always, I think, honest about himself and his flaws. The public refused to hear about those flaws from me, and therefore deprived themselves of his greatest example. Lincoln was not always able to under-stand himself—his superstition, his hypos—but he never evaded mistakes he made. I believe he tried to teach me this directly with his story about drinking and wrassling in New Orleans, but I avoided for years what Lincoln told me on his last day in Springfield. I disregarded for too many years the example of my teetotaler partner. When he quit his yarning voice back then and became earnest about what drinking did to a man's brains, I should have listened to him. Fortunately, my brains had not been bounced beyond recovery by demon rum. With their application and a strong measure of Lincoln's will, I stopped drinking in early 1881. Although I had some setbacks and relapses, by the end of the year I was sober for good. "Welcome back, William," Anna said at Christmas. No mulled hard cider to celebrate, but it was the happiest holiday I can remember on the farm. Somehow Anna had bought us each an orange, and we ate them Christmas morning with her sourdough bread and honey.

Temperance did not mean I no longer failed. In 1882 I ran as a Democrat for the Illinois legislature and lost. In 1883 I employed a lecture agent from Pennsylvania and hoped to make money on a tour of large cities but ended up speaking in small towns for little profit. In that year I allowed another Lincoln biographer, Isaac Arnold, to visit me, listen to my rec-ollections, and read my trove of documents. Arnold's middle name was Newton, and Arnold had the same bare chin but a lot less hair than the scientist. He also lacked old Newton's gravity, for Arnold asked a lot of silly questions: What time did Lincoln get up in the morning? What did he eat? "Anything put in front of him. His trouble was on the other end. He was fearful constipated." Arnold said he couldn't use that fact. Could Lincoln sing? The answer to that one was "Can a jackass whistle?" "Could Lincoln dance?" he asked me in a letter. My reply: "Could a sparrow imitate an eagle? Barnum could make more money on Lincoln's dancing than he could on Jumbo." These questions were what Lincoln biography had descended to—trivial entertainment you might find in a newspaper. I suggested to Arnold that he ask, "Did Lincoln love women?" But Arnold was up in years and refused to take my bait. Lincoln's passion was the subject every biographer avoided, as if the spirit of the times herself, Queen Victoria, had not birthed nine children. When Lincoln was in the White House, the newspapers all laughed over little Tad and wept over Willie, but now that both children and parents were dead no one dared discuss how those children "got begat," as Lincoln would say.

After the very proper Arnold had a man copy some of my documents, Arnold swore to fully acknowledge all my assistance. He was an abolitionist from way back and a prominent lawyer up in Chicago, so I trusted his word. But he died before his book was published, and I was barely mentioned. Though I ought to have been angry, I lacked the energy for it. I had become accustomed to betrayal, not resigned to it but also not surprised. Besides, I probably should have guessed I would be betrayed by the man who wrote a book on Benedict Arnold. I finally decided that I received little credit because my answers to Arnold's insignificant questions were too much like the answers Lincoln would have given.

When I told Anna that Arnold had died, she merely nodded and said, "At least his book will come out." After his biography finally reached me, I told her about receiving almost no credit.

"You are too trusting," she said. "You should have made Arnold sign a contract like Lamon did."

"I wasn't charging Arnold anything."

"You are too trusting and too generous when Lincoln is involved. It's a bad combination. Didn't he charge for his legal advice?"

"Of course."

"So should you for your biographical advice if you're not going to write a book you can sell."

"It's too late now."

"To charge a dead man, yes. But not to write the book. Arnold's proves a market still exists."

"To market, to market, to sell a fat pig. Home again home again, jiggety jig."

"That's the spirit. If Lincoln sold hogs in New Orleans, you're not too pure to sell a book, are you?"

"My book is probably too impure. But you've heard most of my Lincoln stories, Anna. Maybe you should write it. You will bring an objective eye to the president."

"I might write the Democratic Lincoln, a logroller rather than rail-splitter, a vulgar pretender to Douglas's rightful throne, a man who freed the slaves only to have more bodies to throw into his unnecessary war."

I was laughing. "You can say all these things after so many years married to me?"

"Actually, I believe I would imagine up a pure Christian Lincoln to market, as the reverend novelist Holland did. Yes, and a gentle Mary Todd, for it's women who read books."

"Yes, yes," I laughed harder. "Now that you have experience shoveling manure in the barn you're prepared to write 'The Happy Life of Abraham Lincoln.' I'll take charge of the garden."

"No thank you. I wouldn't trust you in my vegetables. You know what Lizzie overheard neighbor Patrick say, 'The only thing Herndon can raise is hell.'"

"You know I don't drink anymore. Not near your vegetables, and not away from home."

"I do, and that's the reason you should write the 'damned' book."

Even my Presbyterian wife had taken to calling my biography "damned." It was like the Wandering Jew, forever in progress. Or like a bond one could not redeem for cash. Or like one of the bills Lincoln refused to collect. He never sued for payment. Anna liked to provoke me as Lincoln used to, but she was not so forgiving and had a long memory, for the debt was now almost twenty years old. The book that began as a "mission" to tell "necessary truths" about the Lincolns had turned into a necessary commodity for the Herndons.

Chapter Fourteen

In 1884 I rented a new office, moved my Lincoln documents, and took a law partner, G. W. Murray, a young Democrat, but my attempt to reenter legal practice soon ended when I realized I could not hear my clients and could not read the small print of statutes. One day I just up and disappeared from the office like Raymond in New Orleans. But through all these disappointments, my spirit stayed strong, and I never went back to the bottle. My legs were shorter than Lincoln's, but I kept plodding on. Like him, I trusted my mind and education would, as he used to say even in the White House, "git" me some success.

It was coincidence, not causality, but after I stopped drinking I started corresponding with Jesse Weik. That correspondence and then our conversations when he moved from Indiana to Springfield restored my interest in the biography. Jesse was twenty-four and a graduate of Asbury University when he first wrote to me. He was a Republican and member of the Indiana bar in Greencastle when he was appointed as a pension agent to investigate disability claims by Civil War veterans and was dispatched to Springfield. Jesse was interested in Lincoln and came to visit my office, where we rummaged through some of my old biographical materials. Jesse is almost as tall as Lincoln but has a small head and is already portly, an odd looking young man who could benefit from some plowing and harrowing at Fairview. He moves slowly, and the day we met spoke carefully. Like me, Jesse was in poor health and several years later resigned from his appointment to become a writer. He proposed that we collaborate on a Lincoln essay for *Harper's Monthly*. I told him unreliable Herndon's name on his essay would spoil its chances, but I agreed to give him information.

Although other biographers I helped ignored my knowledge, wrenched it around against Lincoln, or failed to credit it, I trusted Jesse. Young, educated, and respectful, Jesse may have reminded me of myself when I became Lincoln's Billy. Whatever the cause, Jesse's interest stimulated the most writing I had done in many years. Between October of 1885 and January of 1886, I wrote him thirty-five long letters about Lincoln. I was like the lazy Sangamon become a flood. I was excited without being agitated, writing freely about and for Lincoln, not against some person or force that oppressed me. Here is a sample:

"Had this great man been of an ardent temperament, with swift and strong volumes of rich blood pouring through his brain, had he been impulsive, quick to think and quick to act, rashly running before the complete development of individual ideas into national ideas, marching with banners hastily before his people, blindly grasping at the trend and drift of things, hungry and longing for a quick end of the national quarrel, groping his way before ideas and facts, this great nation would have been two governments this day. His feeble and low circulation, this irritability which slowly responded to stimuli, this organism with herculean strength, not having much wear and tear about it, by nature conserving its forces, this great man with a great heart and greater head, with a sublime patience and an endless endurance, saved the nation from division and consequent ruin."

Why, I wonder now, was I unable to summon this kind of enthusiasm when I tried to begin my biography so many years ago in Springfield? Not that the fervor and tumble here could or should be maintained throughout a book, but this excitement would have started me on my way. Though perhaps not on the right way. Just as it was too early in those years to reveal certain sensitive facts about Lincoln, maybe it was too early for a rampant Billy to recognize the value of Lincoln's "sublime patience." That was his wisdom. My own has been slower to develop, retarded by too much combat. Much older and less spontaneous now, I realize Lincoln's "slowness" made him the thoughtful statesman. He always seemed to be Old Abe. It was a role that gave him time to think, to ruminate like an old cow chewing her cud. The letters to Weik inspired me to chew over Lincoln again and to remember new things about him that came with a surprising clarity. I might have distrusted my memory of events three decades in the past, but the gush of my recollections warranted their authenticity. I felt my two brains were working together: a young one supplying past perceptions, an old one reflecting with late-arriving wisdom.

Thinking about my thinking and my memories then, I recall now how much Lincoln was concerned, even at an early age, that he be remembered. We were going to Petersburg one day after the Compromise of 1850 strengthened the Fugitive Slave Act. Lincoln was in an especially gloomy mood and deeply regretted that he could not rouse and stir up the nation. He said, "How hard it is to die and leave one's country no better than if one had never lived."

I said something like, "We have time yet, Mr. Lincoln."

"Time and the times are agin us, Billy. In fifty years, our names won't be remembered any more than the names of these horses."

"What about Sam Patch?"

"Stonewall's horse? We need to perform heroic deeds to turn nags into immortal steeds."

Lincoln liked to mimic exalted poetic speech and mix it in with homely language. We were the nags, not the steeds.

"'Some things can be done as well as others.' That's what jumping Sam used to say. I suppose that's why Jackson named his horse for the daredevil.

"I ain't hoping to be remembered as a fool in a barrel," Lincoln said. "I want to be known for 'some thing' worthy of respect and admiration. But I feel fate is opposed."

Though I have wanted to do my part for my friend's memory, I never quite understood what in 1850 seemed outsized ambition. By then Lincoln had come a long way up from Thomas Lincoln's laborer. Perhaps Lincoln felt that future fame was therefore not beyond him. He desired immortality though he could not believe in either of the Christian ways to achieve it: by Calvin's fate or Luther's faith. I had no such ambition in 1850 or now. Being mayor of Springfield and improving my fellow citizens' circumstances were enough in the immortality line for me. But Lincoln, despite his public humility, leaned toward Shakespeare's tragic heroes, even if they died in the end. Their lines were the ones he remembered. Lincoln's death was not a tragedy. It did not stem from some fatal flaw, but had he been willing to practice law and raise his children in Springfield he would not have been in Ford's Theatre that night. If Lincoln had survived, he might have said that the fate that brought him out of Kentucky also took him to the Peterson house across from the theater.

When I was writing my letters full of memories to Weik, Anna remarked on the change in my mood. I did not mention the oil I was using late into the night was illuminating correspondence, not my biography. The letters were more than enough for Jesse's essay, so I suggested he use the material for a short book on Lincoln. He was excited by the prospect, and I continued to write him lengthy letters with everything that I remembered about Lincoln, from the way he ate an apple to how he rose from a chair to his worries about his possible illegitimacy. I went to town and spoke with old friends of mine and Lincoln's and reported those conversations to Jesse. I admitted that Lincoln was an enigma, but I told Jesse his responsibility was to report Lincoln's contradictions so that his real character be known. Since Mary Todd Lincoln had died in 1882, Jesse should feel free to describe her influence on Lincoln's ambition and his domestic unhappiness. In addition to my letters, I packed up the loose materials that made up the bound "Lincoln Record" I sold to Lamon and sent them to Jesse in Greencastle, where he had returned after resigning from his government position.

Gradually the short book that I suggested Jesse write became our lengthy book. I lacked the energy to organize all the materials and write out everything that needed to be in a full biography, and Jesse had no firsthand knowledge of Lincoln, so we signed a contract to collaborate and share profits, which pleased Anna. While Jesse was trying to add to my knowledge with research of his own among old-timers in Indiana who might remember Lincoln, I was still trying to fight off bill collectors. I borrowed small sums from Jesse against our royalties. When the ten- and twenty-dollar "advances" were not sufficient, I borrowed one hundred dollars from him, putting up all the papers I sent him as collateral.

In the fall of 1886, I sold some of my Lincoln "relics," including a desk from our office, to the "Lincoln Memorial Collection." Later I was paid a paltry sum to go to Chicago in December and January of 1886 and 1887 to be the "curator" of the "museum" on Market Street—actually sales clerk in the store, someone who could swear to the authenticity of the objects. Some I recognized, some might have come from Lincoln's home, and some may have come from the attics of the two men who started the "Memorial." Very few visitors put down their cash, though some of the younger ones enjoyed my stories about Lincoln and life in Springfield before the war. One young woman asked, "Did you fight Indians when you were a young man?"

"No, but when I was five an Indian did come into our yard and hold a knife to my mother's scalp."

"And what about Lincoln. Did he fight Indians?"

"He served three times in the Black Hawk War, and the only time his pistol was fired was by accident."

"So are there still Indians down there now?"

"Young lady," I had to tell her, "Springfield is the capital of Illinois. The Indians are gone, and so are the buffalo. Perhaps you are thinking of Indianapolis, which is in Indiana."

To these Chicagoans, I was one of those original Settlers who had shouted me down at their barbecue or, worse yet, I was an antique curio like some of the furnishings. Just two decades after his death, Lincoln had gone from martyred saint to object of nostalgia, representative not of heroic moral action but of primitive prairie life. I had gone from ambitious biographer to poorly paid shill for Lincolnania. Sitting in the store, waiting for customers, I wondered: if Lincoln had completed his second term, would he have returned to practice law in Springfield? After eight years in Washington, he might have moved to Chicago, practiced corporate law, and enjoyed the big city life he'd grown accustomed to. Mary might have insisted.

Lincoln as saint, Lincoln as furniture—both denied Lincoln as passionate progenitor. How he would laugh now at how far "ahead" of him I had gotten with my nine heirs. Distraught by the death of Willie, Lincoln was "saved" from the death of his poor tongue-tied Tad six years after the assassination. Now only Robert carried on Lincoln's name and, knowing Robert, I believed it would be the name, not the man, that would most concern Robert. "Father Abraham." "Martyred Emancipator." "Savior of the Union." Robert could preserve every one. The Herndon children were all alive. The irony is this: if the adults are included with Anna and the children, each will inherit just enough land to plant a substantial garden, graze a cow, and grow enough corn to buy a new bonnet or cap every year if there is no drought and not too much rain.

CHAPTER FIFTEEN

While I was in Chicago, Lincoln's adopted heirs, his former secretaries Nicolay and Hay, were serializing their biography in the *Century*. I was pleased to see they preserved Lincoln as a moral exemplar against slavery, but the man was often lost among all the historical upholstery and social frippery with which the "boys" surrounded him. Jesse was alarmed at this competition and expected me, I think, to be angry at these insiders. I was nervous that we would be Hollanded or Lamoned or Arnolded, but soon I realized—and wrote Jesse—that Nicolay and Hay would be gilding over "the Ann Rutledge story, L's religion, L's insanity, the facts of L's misery with Mary Todd." The boys were experienced in foisting deceptive documents on the public. Nicolay admitted to me Lincoln wrote no more than a half dozen letters a week. Nicolay and Hay wrote the rest, and Lincoln signed them without reading. Now there was trust, but I was sure as salt that Lincoln did not trust those young lackeys with his recollections of New Orleans. I also knew that Hay was a close friend of Robert's, who refused me access to the presidential papers he controlled. I could tell Robert had allowed the boys into those papers and would demand reverence in return. I knew both of the secretaries back in Springfield during the first presidential campaign. Nicolay had some spine to him, but Hay was a climber like Mary Todd and he would bend Nicolay to satisfy Robert. So I assured Jesse that the secretaries would be "handling things with silken gloves and a 'camel hair pencil'; they do not write with an iron pen." But Hay and

Nicolay were receiving generous attention and threatening to exhaust interest in Lincoln with their many volumes. Even if they would censor themselves, the secretaries presented a conflict I had to, in Anna's words, run toward and run fast. Jesse and I had to complete our book, so on August 1, 1887, I borrowed the train fare from Jesse and went to Greencastle.

Jesse and I settled into a very hot room above the bakery owned by his father and wrote every day, sometimes twelve or fourteen hours. I would write essays on various subjects— Lincoln the lawyer, Lincoln's domestic life—and Jesse would revise these essays into chapters. I wanted the book to be organized by topics to emphasize its analytic purpose, but Jesse insisted on what he called a "pure narrative style." Using my interviews and letters, he wrote some chapters himself and organized the chapters into a unified story. Since Jesse kept all of our working papers and edited everything, it is impossible now for me to remember exactly how much he wrote and how much I wrote, but I was often displeased with his expression and editing. I remember one sweaty night we quarreled over the following sentence that came after my description of Lincoln's courtship of Mary Owens: "We have thus been favored with the lady's side of this case, and it is fair that we should hear the testimony of her honest but ungainly suitor."

"That's not me, Jesse."

"It's legal language."

"Not in any court Lincoln or I were ever in. It sounds like what a lady novelist would imagine a courtroom was like. And what about the 'we'? The rest of the book uses 'I.'"

"It's a figurative 'we.'"

"It should be a literal 'I.' The whole thing sounds artificial to me. Arch. Lincoln and I used to read some Pope, you know. I don't like to see prewar life treated in a mock heroic style."

Jesse said he would revise this and similar passages, but somehow they turned up in the proof and ended up in the final version. It seemed he and the "Memorial" businessmen shared a belief that the "antique" would sell. I, too, wanted to sell, and yet the tone Jesse took toward history that he was too young to know rankled. He also put my Spencerian analysis of Lincoln's mind, which should have been at the beginning, at the end of the book. "Readers want a good story, not science, in a biography," Jesse told me. "Now you sound like Lincoln," I told him. Readers wanted story, I wanted readers, and Jesse had a lot more literary education than I did, so I deferred and tagged on my analysis at the end.

When I left Greencastle in early September, Jesse asked, "So now we have everything?"

"Everything that those readers of yours want," I told him.

"You have interviews with informants you haven't given me?"

"No, no more interviews. But I can't tell you everything that Lincoln told me, not now."

"Why not?"

"Look at the ruckus I caused with Ann Rutledge, and she was a pure maiden. I've been cursed by readers for too long. I don't want them angry with me, and I don't want to be angry with them, even if they are fools. You'll just have to trust me about this, Jesse."

Almost none of Lincoln's jokes and stories were in the manuscript. He knew when he could get away with telling them, and so did I. We might have included Lincoln's story about drinking in New Orleans, but not the one that follows, not in a Lincoln biography. But this book is my autobiography, and I will take the blame so the story from my notebook can be told. I believe it's necessary to understand something fundamental about Lincoln's character. I place this story about trust here, rather than earlier, because, I suppose, even now I can't trust the response of those readers Jesse favored. The occasion was when I was mayor of Springfield and trying to get the bars and bordellos moved out of the town limits. Lincoln resisted legislating personal morals, so when he started this story I thought it was going to be one of his anecdotes illustrating a political position or maybe just another featherbed yarn.

"We got whorehouses besides the capitol building?" Lincoln asked. "I've never been asked in."

"That's because you're out on the circuit or cooped up at home in the evenings."

"So you're worried Springfield is going to turn into New Orleans, Billy? They got more down there than you can shake your stick at. I believe the city government gets a share of the profits, so the cribs are a source of civic pride. And a reason to ride that damn flatboat with shitting hogs for near a month. Anyways, since you're a married man I reckon it's proper for you to hear something instructive that happened to me down South. Raymond wanted to make sure me and Gentry got the benefits available in 'The Swamp.' Gentry was afeared of carrying some disease back up the river. I'd watched plenty of animals thrusting on the farm, and I was in heat down there in the South, but I warn't too sure of how it would go with a paid girl. Raymond assured me New Orleans girls had experience with Kaintuck virgins, so he took us to a place he knew where the girls was 'tight and clean.' He directed me to the madam upstairs. 'Just like the rum,' Raymond says, 'you pay by the shot if you got more than one in you.' I says, 'I've been saving up my spunk and my money. You and Gentry best not wait for me.'"

Lincoln stopped his telling at this point and said, "Waal, since you married young and went on a honeymoon, I reckon you know what happened next, Billy."

I said, "I've never been to a prostitute, Mr. Lincoln, but my Mary did have some second thoughts on our wedding night."

Lincoln laughed and said, "Hoors don't have no second thoughts. Just second helpings if you can jingle up the cash."

Lincoln selected a girl, and they went into this small bedroom where she took his pants off. He said—though he was probably making this up—she admired his tall man's "steering oar."

"She went to handling it," Lincoln said, "and it stretched out longer than I could ever pull it myself, so she upped her skirts, flopped back on the bed, and said, 'Do your best, farm boy.' But just as I was about to, that Kaintuck hardwood turned soft as a boiled carrot. She handled it some more, agin it softened up. 'Relax, big boy,' she said, but it just warn't going to git in. 'This your first time, boy?' 'I reckon so,' I said. And she tossed back at me, 'I "reckon" we can fix that.' Waal, she got down on her knees like one of them Catholics in church and put it in her mouth. Before I could say the Lord's prayer in thanks, I was shooting off nineteen years of spunk, half in her mouth, half on the floor when she jerked away. 'You supposed to warn me flat boy,' she said, 'that gonna cost you extra.' I apologized and paid her what she asked, but I estimated I didn't have nothing left for a second shot. When I went downstairs, Gentry and Raymond were still there. Raymond was grinning, so I reckon he kind of knew that it would be quick and not too expert.

"But I had this big smile on my face, and Gentry said, 'You shore don't look like you got no disease.'

"'You can come back with me tomorrow night and try it yourself. My girl's name is Emmy.' I didn't tell him about my softwood, but Gentry still never did work up the courage."

"What about you," I asked, "did you go back?"

"Two more times. I wanted to do right by that young lady."

"And those fabled thirteen inches of yours," I said, "she didn't have a problem with all that flatboat wood prodding her?"

"Waal, Billy, she said it was a right lot easier to put it up in her hair hole than take it down her throat halfway to her stomach."

I laughed at that tall part of the tale, but I was curious about Lincoln's failure. "What made you go soft? Was it your conscience squeezing you?"

"I warn't thinking of no preacher, if that's what you're asking. It was like wrasslin' after drinking rum. I warn't myself at first. I'd lost my trust. Thar's your first conscience before the preachers get into it. Those next two nights I jist trusted my body to do what bulls and stallions do. I had my confidence and I had my thirteen inches."

"Did you have your money?" I asked, remembering a story Speed told about Lincoln being short of money with a girl in Springfield.

"Ho, Billy. That Emmy enjoyed my hardwood so much she didn't charge me the last night."

Lincoln hated anyone having the last word on one of his jokes or stories, so he surely made up this ending. But he hated even more losing his trust in himself. With this story, I think he was implying that if I trusted myself I would not be trying to move some of our most successful businesses out of town. When he went off the tracks over his broken engagement to Mary Todd, I know he was tortured as much by failing to trust himself as he was by his guilt. He had made a decision to be done with her but did not hold to it. He wrote to Speed that with Mary Todd he lost "the gem" of his character and could not "trust myself in any matter of much consequence." During our interview, Mary Todd told me her husband was a very stubborn man, but not stubborn enough in those days. I believe it was that failure of self-trust, even more than the prospect of living with Mary Todd, that gave Lincoln the hypo and made him as crazy for a while as the woman he married.

At the time Lincoln told me this story, the voters in Springfield trusted themselves to stay away from the prostitutes but not from the doggeries, which had to move. But only for the year I was mayor. After that citizens trusted in their virtue with both girls and grog in town. I never visited the girls, but I was well acquainted with the grog in the years to come.

Chapter Sixteen

I was right, of course, when I told Jesse some things could not be included in the biography if we wanted readers to have a good clean road. That brothel story was obvious. The response to other material we did put in surprised us. When Jesse finished editing our manuscript, he asked my old friend—and Lincoln's friend—Leonard Swett to look it over. The first chapter included information I had turned up on Lincoln's parents: that his mother Nancy Hanks was probably illegitimate, that no record of her marriage to Thomas Lincoln existed, and that Lincoln—as he told me himself—might have been the son of a man named Enloe, not Thomas Lincoln. Swett insisted that most of this material about Lincoln before he was born should be excised or made vague if the book was to succeed. For decades I had fought to tell everything I knew about Lincoln. I was not too old to be angry, but I could not fight any longer, not about Lincoln's family because my family could not afford my principles. Here is what I wrote to Jesse: "We need not, nor must we lie. Let us be true as far as we do go, but by all means let us bow to the inevitable. If the people will not take the truth, let the crime rest on them and not on our heads. The first chapter will have to be changed, rewritten, modified, gutted." My closing words were, "Success is what we want. We want no failures."

In July of 1888, Jesse sent the final copy of the manuscript to a New York agent, Mrs. Gertrude Garrison, who agreed to represent it. No reputable New York publisher would take it on. Despite my urging, I learned later, Jesse had not "gutted" the first chapter about paternity! The manuscript was therefore found offensive, even called "obscene" by editors. I had no idea the publishing world of New York was peopled by virgins and prudes. Mrs. Garrison eventually sent it to a Chicago firm, Belford, Clarke and Company, that had a reputation for specializing in spicy books by women writers or men posing as women writers. Because our biography was sure to offend some readers, Belford, Clarke was enthusiastic about publishing it with the first chapter intact. But when the manuscript was edited, Belford, Clarke changed its mind and expurgated many passages about Lincoln's early life. Jesse and I were both confused by and angry at the change of direction, but I felt nothing could be done at that stage of the book and at that stage of my life on the farm. The constant reversals and misfortunes almost convinced me of Lincoln's belief in fate. Again I wrote Jesse, telling him to accept the censorship: "Bear in mind that I am first for the dimes, second for the dimes, third for the dimes, and as to glory if it comes let it come."

Herndon's Lincoln: The True Story of a Great Life was published in three volumes in June 1889. Although the old curse of impropriety sometimes marred the reviews, most—in newspapers around the North, in monthly magazines such as *Harper's*, the *Nation*, and *Atlantic*—were positive. I told Anna to pick out her washing machine. When the volumes reached me, I tore open the package and showed them to her without looking at them.

"At last, at last, William. You have done it."

"Jesse and I have done it."

"But this is your book, the book."

Anna admired the leather binding and opened the first volume. I took up a pen to write a dedication to my long-suffering wife.

"What is this?" she asked, and pointed to the title page, which read "By William H. Herndon and Jesse William Weik."

I was astonished, wordless as the moment James Plumley told me Lincoln had been assassinated. My name was in slightly larger font, but there was Jesse's name as coauthor! It appeared so in the proof, and I wrote Jesse that I would never approve. I could not even if I wanted to, I told him, for the book was written throughout in the first person singular. But I had allowed Jesse to correspond with our agent and to deal with the publisher. I trusted him to make my final revisions, which he ignored, and to accept the designation of "Editor" on the title page. If there were to be "glory," I would have to share it.

I told Anna all of this, and she said flat out, "Jesse lied. It was a lie to make himself an author."

Like Lincoln, Anna hated lying. It made her speechless for a moment, and then she continued: "Without Jesse you might not have written *Herndon's Lincoln*, but without you he never would have written more than that local newspaper article he sent you. What did you used to say about you and Lincoln and reading?"

"At Lincoln and Herndon, I did the reading and he did the thinking."

"Here you did the thinking and Jesse did the editing. Why did he lie and put on his name as author?"

"Jesse is ambitious. He doesn't want to practice law. He wants a career as a writer. Being a coauthor helps chug him along I suppose."

"I still don't understand, not this outright lying."

"Jesse didn't know Lincoln, didn't love him, had no real loyalty to him. Jesse's interested in publishing first, money second, and Lincoln third. That's why he included material I didn't want and left out material I did."

"But to betray you like this, William? After you have done so much for him. Why?"

"I don't know. Maybe because I owe him money. He's been sending money as an advance on my share of the royalties."

"I know. But how much money?"

"Around $600."

"You never told me it was so much."

"I trust the royalties will easily cover the loans."

"No, William. No. Here is what you do: you write Mr. Jesse William Weik and tell him that you're charging him 'around $600' for the honor of being 'coauthor' of a book he couldn't have dreamed up in a thousand years."

Anna was angrier than I was at Jesse, perhaps because I had become accustomed to betrayal, maybe because she had never been betrayed by one of our children. And she had not seen Jesse scribbling away in that hot Greencastle room every day, avid and dedicated to the project, if not exactly to Lincoln. I felt Jesse was acting out a story that Lincoln and I knew well. Robert always kept his father at a distance, until he was dead. My Natty chose to work on Chicago streets rather than farm with his father. I rebelled against my father's Democratic Party politics. Lincoln fled his father's farming as soon as he could and refused to attend his father's funeral. That occasion led to one of the strangest conversations I ever had with my partner—comic in its misunderstandings, frightening in its resolution. The conversation is another one that doesn't appear in the published biography.

Lincoln came to the office one morning in January of 1851 and announced, as if he'd just lost a stolen hog case, "My father died yesterday." I offered my condolences, looked around for our court schedule, and told him I'd stand in for him if need be. "I'll be in court," he said. "Well, when is the funeral?" I asked. "Tomorrow. I'm not going to Coles County." He went to his couch and started reading a newspaper.

I knew better than to ask him anything direct that day or any day after, but in two weeks or so I edged around to the topic of Thomas Lincoln when a new client by the name of Isaac came to the office. I told Lincoln to take him because of the Biblical connection. After Isaac left, I asked Lincoln, "How did you get your name anyway?"

"From my father, like everyone, Billy."

"No, I mean your first name. It's a long and heavy burden to place on a little child."

"Didn't you give your boy the long name of an apostle?"

"Nathaniel was named after Natty Bumppo."

"Is that someone from your wife's side of the family?"

"Natty Bumppo is the frontier hero in Cooper's Leatherstocking Tales. You should read more novels, Mr. Lincoln."

"Do you know who Terah was?"

"Is that one of the Todds?"

"You should read more of the Bible, Billy. Terah was Abraham's father. He was a wanderer. When Abraham rebelled against him, Terah threw his son into the fiery furnace, but he survived and later left his father behind to die."

"Did your father know all this when he gave you your name?"

"He couldn't read and wouldn't listen to anyone read, so I believe my mother gave me the name to spite him. He'd dragged her around the countryside. She knew him well. She gave him his fate."

If Lincoln chewed tobacco, he would have spit after pronouncing "fate" because it clearly ended our conversation about Thomas Lincoln, who wandered across Kentucky, Indiana, and several parts of Illinois. This "fate" was not one of the silly superstitions Lincoln learned from Kentucky rustics. It rhymed with and was produced by hate. I have always maintained Lincoln was a fatalist, but this spat "fate" was different from the cosmic necessity of the Pope that he used to quote: "Whatever is, is right." This fate was like a curse that Lincoln believed and upheld until and even after his father's death. "With malice toward none," Lincoln said in his second inaugural, but in the office that day fourteen years earlier I heard malice, even malevolence. Never before or after did I hear this hatred from Lincoln, but from then on I knew that beneath his many generosities and frequent jokes my friend was a very hard man, stony, steel. In the Bible, Abraham was willing to kill Isaac. In Springfield that day in 1851, I knew Abraham Lincoln was a man to be feared as well as loved.

Most of the time, though, Lincoln was avuncular, the uncle I never had. Because of our closeness in age, my arguments with him did not threaten paternal authority, and his differences with me never interfered with my affection for this peculiar man. If Jesse considered me an obstructive parent when he put his name on the title page, he might come round some day to seeing me as an eccentric but kindly uncle.

Three months after receiving my "coauthored" copy of the biography, I learned there would be no "dimes" for the Herndons. Belford, Clarke went bankrupt, and we would see no dimes, nickels, or pennies from the book. When I told Anna, the first thing she said was, "Weik found that publisher, didn't he?"

"Mrs. Garrison and he, yes."

"The publisher's bankruptcy is Weik's punishment for betraying you."

Sometimes it was comforting to be married to a Presbyterian. She could be angry and judgmental in my place. I had been crushed by Chicago trusts, why not a Chicago publisher?

"Just like Lincoln at Ford's Theatre," she went on. "At the moment of your great triumph, you are denied your compensation."

"At least the book exists now."

"Bah," she fumed, waving away my "wisdom." She was practical-minded like my law partner but no fatalist.

"It isn't even the book you really wanted to write," she said.

I was silent, and she asked, hoping to spark some anger, "Well, is it?"

"No," I admitted. "I wanted Lincoln to live in the book, a natural man, a Western man, a flatboater and storyteller."

"So, no real Lincoln and no dimes or dollars for us."

I nodded. We were both silent for a minute or so. It seemed longer because I could not think of a thing to say. So many years, so much work, so many failures, and still no dimes and shared glory. Where was the wisdom that could accept this? Anna took both my hands in hers and said:

"It is a great disappointment, William, but I trust you will think of something. You always have. We are not bankrupt, not yet."

"Not yet," I said.

"You didn't send Weik your black notebook along with your other documents, did you?"

"No, I kept the notebook."

"Good," she said, making a writing motion in the air with her right hand. "I'll be your Nicolay and Hay."

"My biographer?"

"No, your secretary."

In the late summer and fall of 1889, trudging the six miles into Springfield, pushing my grocery cart from door to door, and peddling whatever was ripe from the garden, I took stock. I was seventy. Though thirty-seven, Leigh still talked of marrying. Anna was fifty-three and knew no life other than a farmer's wife. Nina, William, and Minnie still lived on the farm. William's health was as bad as mine, and Minnie was only fourteen. I feared we would go bankrupt, they would lose the farm, and have nowhere to live when I was gone. I was not too pure to sell a book and might have sold mine door to door, but all the copies were gone along with the dimes. I might have sold the documents I sent Jesse to the "Memorial Collection," but I owed Jesse too much to get them back. My love of Lincoln and my "mission" of 1865 had put me in twenty-four years of trouble and, now, in debt I had no way to repay. When I had no more vegetables to sell in October, I took Anna's suggestion, took out my black notebook, and began the book you are now reading. During the next months, there was talk of a second expanded edition of *Herndon's Lincoln* or a different publisher buying the rights to it. I continued to correspond with Jesse and hoped for a different publisher. But Jesse had signed the contract with Belford, Clarke. I was too old to get into a protracted litigation with him over my rights to future royalties, and I could no longer afford to split proceeds with Jesse. I had to become a hard and secretive man like Lincoln: write my own book without telling Jesse. I had to become like Jesse, a man willing to betray his mentor, fellow lawyer, and friend. I would collaborate only with my past self and my black notebook, and receive secretarial assistance from my clear-headed and sure-handed wife. I knew the book would be shorter than *Herndon's Lincoln*, but not because important facts were censored. And I know this book will not be accepted by a "proper" publisher, but even if it is brought out by a disreputable company like Belford, Clarke, *Lincoln's Billy* should find its way into the hands of readers who want truthful history and real life. The biographer Isaac Arnold, whose book was released after his death, showed me the way forward to my final words on Lincoln.

PART FOUR

CHAPTER SEVENTEEN

Christians have plagued me since my first lectures. They hated me—and the thought of Lincoln—dismissing the "revealed truth" of their Creator, His Bible, Moses's laws, the virgin birth, the miracles, and the resurrection of the body. Christian apologists spent pages refuting my free-thinking arguments and mocking the new science of Spencer and Darwin that influenced me. From their theology, Christians extracted ethical judgments like clubs from tree branches. From their ethics came their "propriety," as if the eleventh commandment was Refinement. Underneath propriety was the taboo—sex. It seemed strange to me: Christianity had more hold in the Midwest, out on the farms and in the villages, than in Eastern cities despite the fact that many Westerners grew up on farms and saw what occurred in the barnyard. Yet jokes of the kind that Lincoln used to tell were reviled as "barnyard humor," certainly not fit for women to hear though not a single American woman is known to have given virgin birth. Some of these jokes were not even his but reworked from a British book, *Joe Miller's Jests*. Mary Todd Lincoln could flirt and scheme and cheat and rage like the best or worst of men, could show off her plump breasts and give birth to four children, but woe to the man, her husband included, who told an off-color story in her hearing. No man I ever met was more guilty of impropriety than Lincoln, but in his marriage and in his "society" a natural and basic quality of Lincoln was suppressed, and then suppressed again by biographers such as Holland, Arnold, and Nicolay and Hay—and by editors at Belford, Clarke.

If I reported something "improper" in a lecture or essay, the protectors of refinement blamed me. Even the positive reviewers of *Herndon's Lincoln* objected to two pages about the "Chronicles of Reuben," an account by Lincoln in mock Biblical style of a double wedding celebration where—only momentarily and innocently—the husbands were maneuvered into the wrong beds. For describing what Lincoln had written as a very young man, I was called uncouth, coarse, and vulgar. I'm old but not insensitive to insult, so this chapter is my reply to all the self-righteous Christians who made Herndon a pariah and Lincoln a saint.

I suggest proper reviewers spend some time in the courts of Illinois. Lincoln represented a woman who sued a man for slander because he claimed "she has been fucked more times than I've got fingers and toes for damned if it ain't so big I can almost poke my fist in." Another client, Newton Galloway, declared that one William Torrance "caught my old sow and fucked her as long as he could and knocked up my old sow." These sentences and others like them appear in the public record for any citizen or reviewer to read. Any man and, I believe, not a few women can hear language such as this on the streets of Chicago. I have not pumped up these words or Lincoln's stories from what some readers will surely say is the cesspool of my personal decadence. As I wrote to Weik, "Some people are too nice for this material sphere, this muddy globe of ours."

What follows could not possibly appear in *Herndon's Lincoln* if it expected to yield "dimes" or dollars, and what follows will bring me no "glory," but these pages are the truth of Lincoln—the truth about him and the truth from him. Throughout the biography I used "manly" to describe Lincoln as a courageous and fair person. When Anna read the book, she asked, "Does this mean 'womanly' is meek and conniving?" "Male" better describes the adult Lincoln, for he was full of male interest in the female, whether human or not. Joseph Watkins told friends that Lincoln asked him to be informed when one of Watkins's mares was ready to be mounted so he could go watch the stallion at work. A number of my informants agreed that while the teenage Abraham was shy around women, after he left his family and came to New Salem, where he was a clerk and then postmaster, he waited on women and took more notice of them. He was particularly fond of Hannah Armstrong in nearby Clary's Grove, and her husband used to joke that Lincoln fathered one of Armstrong's sons. For some time after his first trip to New Orleans and a later "devilish passion" for a prostitute in Beardstown, which he also told me about, Lincoln worried he had contracted syphilis. I believe this worry affected his courtships, his advances and retreats. He proposed to Mary Owens and then managed to talk her out of marrying him. He proposed to Sarah Rickard, a girl so young she was unlikely to accept. He was engaged to Mary Todd and broke the engagement. His ideal love, Ann Rutledge, died like a woman in a Poe poem before they could be married.

When he and Speed and I, along with other young blades, were sleeping above Speed's store, Speed used to tell a story about Abe the lover. Speed was much more comfortable than Lincoln going to parties where eligible virgins might be courted, but dancing and flirting did not satisfy Speed, so he had a local "girl" he could visit on occasion. Lincoln was new in town and awkward, so he piggybacked, so to speak, on Speed's girl. Well, not exactly a girl. I saw her once, and she was a stout woman of near middle age whose husband had left her. More than once up in Speed's room with Lincoln present, Speed told about Lincoln's first visit to the "girl." The story went like this:

"Lincoln went to see the girl with a note from me, and she agreed to satisfy him. Things went on right. Lincoln and the girl stript off and went to bed. Before anything was done, Lincoln said to the girl, 'How much do you charge?' 'Five dollars,' she said. Lincoln said, 'I've only got three dollars.' 'Well,' said the girl, 'I'll trust you, Mr. Lincoln, for two dollars.' Lincoln thought a moment and said, 'I do not wish to go on credit. I'm poor and I don't know where my next dollar will come from and I cannot afford to cheat you.' Lincoln got up out of bed, and the girl said, 'Mr. Lincoln, you are the most conscientious man I ever saw.'"

When Speed told this story, Lincoln laughed as loud as anyone. I also laughed at Honest Abe in the house of sin; but after I married the true "girl" I loved when my Mary was eighteen and I was twenty-two, I recognized an important difference between Lincoln and me. Lincoln was a single man until the age of thirty-three. He was, as I told Lamon, "a man of terribly strong passions." That he wished to be married and to enjoy the benefits of the featherbed is proved by his active courtships of many women and, perhaps, even partly explains why he would marry a woman he did not love—the most sensual woman, I have to admit, I ever met. I envied Lincoln's physical force and mental powers. The way he joked about my many heirs, perhaps he envied my early start in the marriage chamber and a wife who was not a shrew. Although different in his experience from me, Lincoln was not different from many single men who find women to pleasure them when they cannot find wives to please them.

Physical desire may have been the reason Lincoln and Mary Todd were mishitched like an oxen and donkey, but his coupling in New Orleans had an even more profound effect on Lincoln's whole life. All along while writing this supplement to my biography, I have been considering whether or not I would tell the final secret that follows. Considering and delaying and consulting my conscience, I have concluded that this last material from my notebook is too important—reveals too much about Lincoln's private character and public actions—to suppress. Most of our conversations about New Orleans came early in our partnership when Lincoln was a less careful man than he was once office-seeking and Mary

Todd took hold of him. The following conversation I can date precisely because it occurred when I returned from arguing with Elliott about the Fugitive Slave case. I was ashamed of my brother, but I thought Lincoln should know that a lawyer he knew called him a "nigger-loving amalgamationist." Lincoln was silent, as he often was when addressed. Sometimes it was just silence. This time it was preparation.

"Your wild-haired Douglass says amalgamation would eventually solve the race problem. Everyone and no one would be a Negro. But from a fellow member of the bar and my partner's brother, that's a serious charge."

"It's politics, Mr. Lincoln, speaking through Elliott."

"I expect he's right about us being 'nigger lovers' over here, though we're probably not equal in our affections."

"Maybe just not equal in our public displays and political actions."

"Maybe we're not equal in our experience, either."

"I've never been attacked by slaves on the way to New Orleans or been in a Deep South slave state."

My mentioning New Orleans shifted Lincoln into his old Kaintuck yarning voice.

"It surely is different down thar with colors mixed up together like the rivers that make up the great Mississip. With all them Mexicans and Indians and sailors and Chinese and what they call 'high yallers' tangled up like mangroves, it's hard to tell who's amalgamated and who ain't. I expect even folks as white as you and me walk round with papers attesting to the fact. For all I know, Raymond might have dressed all in white because he was dark underneath. It's damned hard to know who's free and who ain't. I knew the slaves I saw at auction warn't free, not with chains around their necks. But there was also Negroes walking around with high boots and high collars. It's a place of confusions. I still ain't sure if that fortune-teller was a man or a woman. No sir, Billy, New Orleans ain't New Salem. Or Springfield. It ain't even Chicago. Now that I been around these states some, I figure New Orleans is the future. Down there it's even hard to tell who's a man and who's a boy. I came up behind this shorty juggling, and I thought that was some feat for a child. Turned out he was one of them dwarfs and even homelier than me. Around the wharves children in short pants walked about whistling up business for the brothels. Do you remember me telling you about that girl who called me 'farm boy,' 'big boy,' and 'flat boy' when I couldn't keep my old horny straight?"

"How could I forget, Kaintuck?"

"Waal, on my second trip down there, when I couldn't find Raymond or his house, I could find the whorehouse right easy. This ain't a pretty story, Billy, but maybe now's the time for you to hear it. I didn't stop at the bar for no rum. I went upstairs, and the same madam was sitting in her little room. I do believe she had the same clothes on, all dressed in black like a proper abbess. I told her I'd like to take a shot with Emmy, and I'll be damned if that white madam didn't say the same thing as the black butler where Raymond had a house: 'She's gone.'

" 'I don't reckon you know where,' I said, just like the big boy Emmy called me.

" 'No other house,' she said, 'she got knapped.'

"The farm boy says, 'She was kidnapped?'

" 'No, son, she was pregnant. That French letter must have come unsealed. It's the prostitute's curse. For most women, it's the monthlies, my girls are happy to see 'em come on.'

" 'How long ago did she leave?'

" 'I got so many girls passing through here, you can't expect me to know that. Two years ago, maybe three.' "

Lincoln stopped there for a moment and then continued.

"It pains me to say it, Billy, but you can't always trust old Honest Abe. That Emmy never did call me 'flat boy.' No, not 'flatboat boy' either. She said, 'Do your best, white boy.' "

I suppose I should have been shocked, but isn't that what white men did in the South? Have intercourse with Negroes. Isn't that what Stephen A. Douglas, in his debates with Lincoln, said abolitionists wanted to do? Southern slaveholders, who had been impregnating their slaves for centuries, accused Northerners of wanting the same "privilege." I knew Lincoln expected some response from his abolitionist friend, so I asked a stupid question.

"Was she a free black like the women Raymond said worked for him?"

"She was light skinned, but I can't know that any more than I know where Raymond and his help went to. But I can tell you this, Billy: I've never got free of her. Never been free of the possibility that Emmy was carrying my child. I never got quit of the probability that the child would be a slave. Cousin Hanks likes to say it was seeing a slave auction down there that made me disgusted with slavery. Hanks wasn't there. It was recognizing that I might have fathered a slave that disgusted me. Disgusted me with slavery and myself. So, you see, your brother might be right. I might be an amalgamationist."

"That's just your old superstition at work, Mr. Lincoln. Look at the odds. Consider how many customers Emmy had. Think like a lawyer: that madam may not have been telling the truth."

" 'Might' is plenty strong enough when slavery of a child is involved, Billy. 'Might' is like a mite that has burrowed down so deep in my conscience I'll never get free of the guilt."

Lincoln laughed. Now I was shocked.

" 'Honest Abe,' " he said. "Folks call me Honest Abe, but when they ask me why I'm against slavery, I don't tell them. I tell them it's bad law, bad policy. Or I fall back on the Christians I don't believe in and say, 'It's a moral curse on the land.' Conscience makes me a coward, as Will says. And adds on the guilt of not telling the truth. People ask me, 'Why

do you look so sad? What has cast such a shadow on you?'
I can't answer true: 'The Negro.' "

Then the silence was silence, not preparation for something more. I had to intuit the meaning of Lincoln's face. He did not look me in the eye, as if he were soliciting my trust. He cast his eyes down, as if ashamed, but he also seemed relieved as if he were one of those New Orleans Catholics who just stepped out of a confession box. I assumed that relief was Lincoln's reason for telling me this story he knew I'd find shameful.

Because I knew this secret about Lincoln, because I knew how personally slavery affected him, I did, as my Mary said, try to "keep his feet to the fire," press him to adjust his political positions to what was in his heart. I never asked him why he chose the Negro woman to take his virginity. Perhaps at the time the Kaintuck farm boy felt it somehow less sinful to mate with a Negro. Maybe he took his lead from Raymond or was seduced by those Congo Square drums. I never mentioned the connection between slavery and prostitution, the buying and renting of flesh. After the Emancipation Proclamation, I wondered if his "shadow" lifted or if he saw it as responsible for the war that took so many lives of whites and Negroes, North and South.

Lincoln never implied that my constant pressure to end slavery influenced him. I can say only that I tried to move him faster than he wanted to go toward abolition. That was my mission when he lived. But Lincoln knew best, as history has demonstrated. He had traveled more than I and heard voices from all over the Union. I talked to him. He listened to crowds. I wanted to be a force, he wanted to be a president. Lincoln calculated and temporized, and there were times when I resented him. But he knew just how far he could go against slavery and still be elected. He was between the abolitionists and the Copperheads, just as he was between his idealistic law partner and his materialistic marital partner, just as I have been between readers who want biographies to be true and those who want biographies to be false. But being between made Lincoln president and being slow made him a statesman.

When Lincoln told me about the Negro prostitute in New Orleans, he did not need to say our conversation had to be a secret. Fornication and miscegenation—these are the worst taboos of our proper Christian nineteenth century and reason I've delayed telling this dark story here. Ever since I recorded our conversation in my black notebook, I have thought it a pity Americans could not know this Lincoln, a man like many men who can "fall" but a man like very few men who lets his failure govern his conscience and afflict his temperament and, eventually, lead him to a sweeping historical act of justice—emancipating the slaves. For years I knew Lincoln was a man steeped in and stooped by guilt—for surviving his mother and his only love, for possibly contracting syphilis, for revealing to the woman he married that he didn't love her—but I never had the courage to reveal the guilt of New Orleans even though I believed that more than anything else it explained the hypos he experienced as long as he lived. Unable to tell this story in my biography, I used John Hanks's suspect tale about the source of Lincoln's disgust: his seeing a "vigorous and comely mulatto" at auction, her flesh being "pinched" by prospective owners. In fact, Lincoln was much more intimate with a "comely mulatto." Lincoln was relieved to tell me his amalgamation story. I am relieved to finally be able to retell it here. Yes, relieved but also guilty.

CHAPTER EIGHTEEN

When Anna finished copying over the preceding chapter, she asked, "Can this story be true, William?"

"Would I make up such a story?"

"No, I mean are you sure Lincoln was telling you the truth?"

"About his disgust with slavery?"

"About the prostitute and child."

"Would any man invent such a shameful story about himself?"

"Waal," she said, imitating my Lincoln, "it ain't one I'd make up, but I reckon I kin imagine a man who loved children atellin such a story." Then she spoke normally, saying, "Didn't he make up a different voice when he was spinning you yarns."

"That was just for fun between us."

"But Mr. Lincoln did like to tell tall tales, and haven't you said several times that he made up parts of his New Orleans stories?"

I sensed where Anna was heading, and it was an unbelievable direction: honest Anna was going to call Lincoln a liar. His trusting Billy had never considered that possibility. For a minute, I was as speechless as that terrible day at the telegraph office.

"He probably made up details to entertain," I managed to say, "but why would he invent this one?"

"I don't know, but didn't you invent a whole conversation with his ghost when you were trying to begin your book?"

Another damned censor was my first thought. Anna was already a collaborator because she helped me remember some of our conversations. One of the pleasures writing this book was recalling together our dialogues from years past, even if Anna often had the best lines. But I wanted no more censors.

"Are you saying I should leave it out?" I asked her.

"Not if it's true, but I'm glad I won't be the one blamed for writing it out."

"It's in your hand. After I've passed, you can take the credit. Mary Todd would."

"I doubt anyone would believe a woman—not even crazy Mary—would write out those last two New Orleans stories."

"Do you believe the final one is true?"

"I trust it is, but if it isn't, it should be. It's the amalgamated Lincoln."

"What do you mean 'amalgamated'?"

"Black and white together, impure and pure fused, immoral and moral, both sinner and redeemed. At the end, William, you've made Lincoln into my Christian."

Except for that last sentence, my new collaborator had Lincoln exactly, a man of fused contradictions. Amalgam is a rare mineral in nature, silver and mercury, and Lincoln was a rare natural man, a silver-tongued messenger in his great addresses. But Anna's questions and comments distressed me and required me to write more, think more, and think more about Lincoln's thinking, what no other biography, including *Herndon's Lincoln*, had adequately done.

Lincoln's story about the prostitute differed from the first time he told it. And it differed from what John Hanks wrote about New Orleans. In court and suspicious, I would have hounded the witness. But at the time I was Lincoln's Billy, still young, perhaps overly respectful, and did not question his story. It fit with what I knew of him in New Orleans and with his conscience. It reassured me that we saw eyeball to eyeball on slavery, even if our experience was different and our mouths could not say the same things. And maybe I somehow wanted to believe that my senior partner was not a paragon of virtue. Possible amalgamation made my occasional benders look fairly innocent.

That was me. But if his story was a tale, what, I wonder now twenty-five years after his death, could have been honest Abraham Lincoln's motive for lying. There was no profit to be gained, the most common reason for our clients' layered lies.

If Lincoln told me his stories about failure—Raymond's and Lincoln's when drinking and when not trusting himself—as generous moral lessons for his young partner, maybe this story about paternity was for himself, a way to strengthen my trust and to tamp down my constant insistence that he come round to my way of thinking about Dred Scott and abolition. Altruism versus selfishness, our old argument.

Or maybe Lincoln told me this story to test my trustworthiness as partner and confidant at a time when my opposition to slavery was becoming more "rampant and spontaneous." If this story about amalgamation got out and then back to Lincoln, he would know the source, and because it was so outrageous he could easily deny it as a fiction invented by his Democratic enemies like Elliott.

After many years together in the office, maybe Lincoln had finally tired of old stories and made up new ones about New Orleans. Perhaps that city stimulated not just his ambition but his imagination, so he invented stories set there not to elicit trust or even to test but simply to tell tales. They seemed to freely and unexpectedly arise like a hypo but the reverse, creative rather than depressive. For the slow-moving and slow-talking Lincoln, telling stories like these provided a feeling of intensity. Stories were vital and vivid like those unrestrained Negro dancers he saw in New Orleans. Perhaps his inventions were "rampant and spontaneous" like his Billy. If true, that would at last make him Billy's Lincoln.

Lincoln could be cruel. In his early days in the law and politics, he liked to "skin" opponents with insulting, sometimes exaggerated, and always anonymous satires he wrote for the local papers. That is how he nearly came to a duel with James Shields. Stories gave Lincoln the kind of power no lawyer or politician or man courting a woman could afford to have, a force not constrained by conscience. He liked to entertain but also shock, to both attract and repel the listener. Maybe he realized his effect and told the New Orleans stories only to me, his junior, an easily affected audience of one.

The more Anna's questions made me think, the darker the mind shaft became. Lincoln could have told me his instructive stories because he didn't trust his young partner to learn from his own mistakes or because Lincoln wanted to prove his own moral superiority. Perhaps it was the hard man Lincoln who told tales, the older man with less than thirteen inches of hardwood who lagged behind his young partner in the marital chamber. If he could not pin me in a rational argument, he could put me on my back with one of his stories. Maybe Lincoln was more a Spencerian man than I'd realized, a biped with a double brain, a six-foot four-inch organism whose fundamental law was dominance, "survival of the fittest" through fiction.

Lincoln could have made up stories as relief, not from hypos as most people thought, but from himself, from always being Honest Abe. If true, I wish he had taught me to lie for release from always being Trustworthy Billy. Lies were all around me—the fabrications of partisan politics, the perjuries of clients desperate to keep or make money, the fantasies of informants who wanted to have a role in Lincoln's biography, the broken promises of my former collaborators—but I never learned, so telling the truth has put me in trouble since Lincoln died.

Speculating about Lincoln's motivations makes me think he might have been upside down. Although he condescended to the novels I sometimes read, perhaps Lincoln was not, as I always believed, organically and helplessly truthful but fundamentally a storyteller who was forced by circumstances, the law, and even politics to become a truth teller. Under different conditions, Lincoln might have become a Twain, a riverboat pilot turned humorist and novelist, or my wives' Poe, a poet turned teller of unreliable tales about horrible guilt. Either would have been a loss to the nation. But if this topsy-turvy Lincoln I have imagined were true, then Lincoln was a loss to himself, betrayed by his ambition and separated from what Emerson would have called his soul. No wonder Lincoln seemed melancholy unless he was making jokes or telling stories. For him, the rest was sadness.

Lincoln picked me as his partner because, he said, he trusted me. Perhaps I should have trusted him less. Or should I have trusted myself less, my love of and loyalty to Lincoln? It is impossible for me to resolve now these questions of truth and trust. A biography and autobiography are not a court of law. Attorney Shields and attorney Lincoln never used their swords, and this book is not the case of dueling lawyers. In my uncertainty, I choose to return to the wisdom of my mentor before I met Lincoln. Most of my books were sold so I could plant and harvest corn, but I kept my optimistic Emerson: "Trust men and they will be true to you; treat them greatly and they will show themselves great." Whatever Lincoln's motives were for telling me stories, I choose to trust him and the truth of those stories. Despite the youthful failures he admitted in his New Orleans stories, he surely showed himself great as a mature man. I trust readers will recognize that nothing I have revealed here about Lincoln diminishes that greatness but only increases it, for this was a man who did not just overcome his humble beginnings, as the legend has it, but overcame his own mind—his superstitions, his hypos, his guilts. And he overcome the tragedies of his personal life—his cursed father, the early death of his mother, the deaths of his sons, the madness of his wife—to become the great statesman who freed the slaves and preserved the Union.

That day in 1865 when I learned that Lincoln would not return to Lincoln and Herndon I wanted to comfort the people who kept asking me, "What do you know, Billy?" I know, from all the earlier attacks on me, that this book will discomfort and dismay many readers, but I also believe the Lincoln here could be a comfort to men and women. They will know the most respected figure of our recent history had the same urges and passions and weaknesses they have.

When *Herndon's Lincoln* was published, those who found it offensive presumed my motivations. I was taking revenge on the president who did not appoint me to a lucrative government post. I was demeaning the great Republican because I had become a Democrat. I was betraying the man who treated me like a son. None was true, but now that I have almost finished this book I do wonder if I should trust myself, for my book may unintentionally create a Billy's Lincoln in my own image—a Kentucky-born freethinking Infidel, a person disgusted by slavery but unembarrassed by sex, a man guilty about surviving a first love and disappointing a wife, a repeat failure who waited long for the success he wanted. I always intended to write a "subjective" biography, but not of me. That is why I relied on my informants, their objective testimony, and did not trust only my own experience of Lincoln, and yet I wonder if my Marymax would now say Abraham Lincoln and William Herndon were both "William Wilson."

Having thought through all these possibilities, I ask myself one final question: If Lincoln did lie to me, would I be free to lie about him? It didn't even matter. It was moot. With no tall tales of my own, I remain Lincoln's Billy, able only to retell Lincoln's stories. Recalling here our lives together has caused me to remember stories by and about Lincoln that I had forgotten. One about New Orleans, though not in my notebook, is, I believe, entirely trustworthy, for Lincoln had nothing to gain by telling it. Because it is about truthful representation, now seems to me the appropriate time to retell it. The occasion was the burial of our friend Hiram Williams, a newspaper editor who amused Lincoln no end, just a week before he was leaving for the White House. Lincoln and I were walking out of Oak Ridge Cemetery, where he was buried four short years later, when he began talking about a cemetery he'd seen in New Orleans. "Saint Louis," I believe he said it was called.

"Alas, poor Hiram. That damn hole always puts a hypo on me ever since I watched my father and cousin Hanks dig my mother's grave. I couldn't bear to be at Ann Rutledge's burial. When we buried infant Eddie, they dug a regular size hole for his child-sized coffin. I had dreams for weeks about him rattling around in all that extra space. Down South they do it better. They want no floating corpses if them levees give way. So they bury folks above ground. Them with the most money build little mansions to stash themselves in like they might be coming back one day. Lesser folks just have a good solid tomb sitting up on the ground."

"I guess these must be the white folks," I said. "Where do they put the Negroes?"

"That I don't know, Billy. Maybe they float 'em out to sea, send 'em back to Africa. But what I was fixing to tell you is some of those mausoleums have big statues outside them. Old Indian killers in bronze are prancing about on their slathered-up horses. But mostly it's religious figures. A popular one is Jesus standing with his hands spread out beside him like he is walking down the aisle and asking for donations. I expect it's Catholics who have his kneeling mother supplicating heaven like she is pleading with a man who got her up the pole and run off. But the statue I liked best was a man lying on his tomb."

"How was he lying?"

"What do you think, Billy? That he was on his belly trying to get up on top of his dead wife?"

"You ever hear the difference between a wife in bed and in a casket?"

"What is it?"

"You have to feed the one in bed."

Lincoln did not laugh. Maybe it cut too close to home. Heading to the White House, Lincoln may have wished he could box up Mary Todd.

"So what did you like about that statue?" I asked.

"He was flat on his back . . ."

"What?" I interrupted. "I can't believe you favored such a statue since you were never put on your back when wrassling."

"Every man is on his back when he's dead. But you keep delaying me from the nib. See, I reckon this feller arranged for his statue before he passed."

"Maybe his family or some admirer commissioned it."

"That's possible, but he must of posed for it because the likeness was exact like one of them old death masks you see in books."

"How could you tell it was exact if you didn't know him?"

"All the details was realistic. His long beard fairly rippled. His nose had little indents for nostrils. The sculptor even left his eyes open. If you got up close and peered down, that feller lying there seemed to be looking at you eye to eye."

"Was his eyeball transparent?"

"Fuck sakes, Billy, are you making jokes now? Listen, I hope to teach you a lesson about a law that ain't in your books. I didn't think about that statue much right then because I was young as a shoat. But now every time I come out here, I remember that statue and think, yes sir, that there statue shows what life is—preparation for how you'll be remembered when you're dead."

"Who was this dead feller?"

"I didn't read the writing on that tomb. Raymond said mayors and such were buried in the mausoleums. Probably my feller was just some rag-ass preacher or ward politician who failed to git his hands in enough pockets to buy himself better lodging for eternity, but he looked fine in marble."

"He might have been a Negro, one of the successful free blacks I hear they have down there."

"You ever seen black marble, Billy?"

"Maybe he was passing. You told me New Orleans was all confusion. A black man pretending to be white would have white marble on his tomb."

"It was surely a white man. Any fool could see that by the likeness."

"But a man might be fooled by the likeness if the sculptor wanted the feller to look white."

"And I'm telling you, Billy, that man and statue was white. It was so lifelike it had the power of a statute."

When Lincoln hesitated just a bit before stating the "nib," his word for the "point," I asked him another riddle.

"You know how a statue and a statute are alike?"

"How?"

"They both get worn out over time."

"You're never going to be worth a shit telling jokes, Billy."

"Speaking of shit, do you know the difference between a lawyer and all other animals? With a lawyer, shit comes out of his mouth. But listen, I want to tell you this story . . ."

Lincoln interrupted me, stopped walking, and turned toward me.

"Not now, Billy. I'm trying to lay down Lincoln's law for you. Here's the nib. Make damn sure what people remember is a good likeness when you're dead."

We walked along silently, so I could take in Lincoln's law. Just as we were about to go through the cemetery gates, Lincoln started laughing to himself and said, "Billy, I'm so damned long they'll have to show me with my knees jacked up to fit me on the tomb."

"And they'll have to tie down that thirteen inches, too."

"Only if old Jeff Davis hangs me, Billy."

"Or you 'hang yourself,' as your Shakespeare says."

I remember that whole exchange very clearly because it was the only time I recall having the last word—even if it was his Shakespeare's coarse pun—on one of Lincoln's stories. Otherwise that conversation was Lincoln. Even as president-elect, he was mournful but scoffing and joking and giving advice and laughing at himself. Every time I go out to the cemetery, I hear my friend's words, as if he were a ghost haunting Oak Ridge.

Thinking back now, I wonder about "Lincoln's law." Did "good likeness" mean an accurate representation or a positive reputation? If it was the latter, why would he have told me the amalgamation story, true or not? If "good likeness" meant accurate representation, I wouldn't need to feel guilty about this book. Maybe Lincoln was speaking more literally, concretely. Lincoln was never satisfied with any of his photographs. He said, "They all make me appear like I've been dead for two minutes." Maybe they were too "lifelike." Marble could smooth out defects. Lincoln overcame many things in his life but never got over his homely face, present before he got his name, before his mother died, before his father made him a slave. The face even seemed older than Lincoln, as if it came from some earlier stage of human development when jaws needed to rip tough meat. He said he once met a woman who told him, "Well, for the land's sake, you are the homeliest man I ever saw!" Lincoln replied, "Yes ma'am, but I can't help that." And the woman said, "No, I suppose not, but you might stay at home." His appearance made him nervous around women and led him to seek out the company of men when possible. Lincoln believed in fate, and his face was his. Whatever stories he told and whatever deeds my friend performed as president were never going to change the fact of his face, not for him. It was a truth hard and cold as marble. To escape that fate, Lincoln had to wait for the sculptors. Then he would have two faces, the one nature gave him mouldering in his casket, the one art gave him shining above the tomb. The statues would be immortal until weather pitted them or hammer-wielding barbarians got after them, knocked off their noses and privates. In the old child's game, paper covers rock. Words cover paper. These pages suffice for me. I crave no marble. One face is enough.

Leaving the cemetery that day in 1861, I felt sorry for the president-elect, just as I did when leaving him at the White House a year later. I feel the same way now, for I never saw him happy after he left the office of Lincoln and Herndon. Washington entombed him, then he came back to Oak Ridge. I go out there about once a year to visit his mausoleum. It's New Orleans style, way above ground and far from the Sangamon where I first saw Lincoln. I like to imagine the vulgar joke he'd make about the jutting obelisk that must be thirteen feet high. He's not lying in marble anywhere. Outside he's standing in bronze, inside he's sitting in bronze. In 1876 a couple of men from Chicago planned to steal Lincoln's remains and hold them for ransom, but now he's buried deep and safe beneath a massive cenotaph. "Waal, Billy," I hear him saying about the ransom plot, "them boys would have been a heap better off kidnapping a live dog than a dead lion." The bronze likenesses are good, I suppose, and I expect metal outlasts marble, but I don't much like the site. It's not honest. There's nothing humble about it. It's grandiose as Lincoln never was. But I still go out there to be reminded of his Kaintuck voice and to remember the stories he loved to tell. Words are what Lincoln left me.

The day we were together in the cemetery, Lincoln said he didn't think much about that statue in New Orleans when he saw it because he was young. I didn't think too much about it when he told me because I was still fairly young. But now I think this: since I started out on my true likeness of Lincoln in 1865, I have let others build my tomb—quote my lectures, use my research, retell my anecdotes, copy my letters, revise my prose. This little book is my own statue on that tomb. Long ago brother Elliott accused me of "egoism." I still deny it because I know this statue is just a small one outside the Lincoln mausoleum in the worldwide city of the dead.

CHAPTER NINETEEN

Whatever errors of intuition and interpretation I may have committed in these pages, at least my style demonstrates, I trust, my ultimate loyalty to Lincoln. He admired the rhymesters Byron, Burns, and Poe, and told me if I ever wrote a novel to put it in verse. Back when we used to discuss poetry in the office, I praised the jagged lines of Emerson and the lengthy lines of Whitman.

"That Whitman looks like me up in New Salem," Lincoln said when I showed him *Leaves of Grass* with its photograph of the poet in open shirt and cocked hat. I asked Lincoln to read "Spontaneous Me" since he called me too spontaneous.

"I thought he looked like a flatboater down in New Orleans," I told Lincoln. "Like you, Whitman spent time there."

"Looks like me but writes like you, Billy. Willy-nilly."

"Thinks and writes like me, Mr. Lincoln. A Free Soiler, I understand."

"He surely does freely soil the page."

"It's good, true American soil, Mr. Lincoln."

"The man does know his dirt and his own 'root,' Billy, but he don't know how to rhyme."

Whitman did rhyme when he wrote about Lincoln's death in "O Captain, My Captain." It was a simple poem like those that Lincoln wrote, so he might have approved. I trust he would approve of my expression here. Looking back over copies of the letters I wrote to Weik, I saw they were sometimes Whitmanian in their effusions and crowded clauses. I was impassioned to be writing about Lincoln again. "Unscrew the locks from the doors! Unscrew the doors themselves from their jambs!" as Whitman wrote in "Song of Myself." Weik disciplined my profusion, but I smelled the musty locked parlor in some of his revisions. Knowing I would have no editor while alive for this book, I disciplined myself. I wanted a prose that could not or would not be tampered with. A prose like Lincoln wrote, a style to prove that late in my life I became a man of few and well-chosen words, "straight and true," as Lincoln used to say, "as a plumb bob to hell."

My secretary, collaborator, and executor has finished copying all that you have read. The remaining sentences—my delayed dedication—I will copy over myself though my hand is shaky. When Anna was done with her handiwork, she—Democrat, Presbyterian, and former Southern sympathizer—said, "Mr. Lincoln was no saint, and he might not have been a hero, but he surely was a good man."

"That's what I've wanted to show Americans since he died."

"You remember how you used to complain about the way Mr. Lincoln allowed his boys to run wild in your office?"

"Sure, they spoiled enough pens to equip four lawyers."

"He let them run free because he believed there might be another child of his in bondage in Louisiana."

To be married to me, Anna has needed to be a strong woman, but she began to cry, which started tears rolling down my own old sunken cheeks. Sometimes skeptical of Lincoln and my dedication to him, at other times reminding me of my former partner, Anna supported me through my biographical travails, calming me like Marymax when necessary, spurring me like Mary Todd when required. I trust that when the time comes for *Lincoln's Billy* to see the light of day that she will weather its certain storms and still support it, and that it will help support her and my children. This book is about Lincoln and me, but it is for them, my last chance to prove Lincoln wrong about altruism. I hope the words here will emancipate my children from their memory of their father as a failed lawyer, failed farmer, and almost failed biographer.

William Herndon died in 1891, less than two years after his biography was published. For facts about his life, I am indebted to David Donald's 1948 biography *Lincoln's Herndon*, though it is strangely condescending. A more balanced and much more recent treatment of Herndon and Lincoln's early life is Douglas Wilson's *Honor's Voice*. Wilson also edited a useful collection entitled *Herndon's Informants*, which presents many of the documents that Herndon and Weik relied on when writing *Herndon's Lincoln*. Herndon's correspondence with Weik and others is available online and is invaluable for intimate details and for Herndon's personal voice. By far the best, most complete biography of Lincoln that I consulted is Michael Burlingame's *Abraham Lincoln: A Life* in two large volumes, published in 2008. For information about New Orleans at the time Lincoln visited, I used Richard Campanella's *Lincoln in New Orleans* although its title is misleading since almost nothing is known about Lincoln's experiences there. Herndon did have two black notebooks in which he kept his most sensitive information, but neither one has turned up in document collections. My Herndon's accounts of Lincoln's recollections of New Orleans extrapolate from what historians do know about Lincoln as a young man and how he talked when telling his stories. Where there are voids in the record about Herndon's life with his family, I have filled them based on what little we know about his wives and children. From his letters, we know that Herndon was widely read, so nineteenth-century writers and works with which he was familiar make small appearances in *Lincoln's Billy*. I have tried very hard to be true to what Herndon knew or could have known when writing this autobiography. Whether or not his reliability can be trusted, readers will have to judge.

I want to thank Jerome Charyn, who first interested me in Lincoln, encouraged me to write about Herndon, and read the manuscript. Thanks also to other readers who commented on and improved the manuscript: Heather and Wayne Hall, Lee Kellogg, Dennis James, Neil Isaacs, and Soren Mrkich.